'Hopefully it won't ⸻
don't need ⸻
Nadia murm⸻
we'll have fo⸻
of you have ⸻
gorgeous gree⸻

A soft sound behind her had her glancing over her shoulder, straight into the eyes in question, which were sporting a definite gleam of amusement.

'Gorgeous green eyes?' Gideon repeated teasingly, and she felt the wash of heat sweep up from her throat and into her face.

'I...' She had to stop to clear her throat, her brain frantically searching for something to say that would minimise the embarrassment of the situation. 'I always talk nonsense to the babies so I don't give them a shock when I touch them.'

His raised eyebrow told her he didn't buy her gabbled excuse, then he laughed, and those gorgeous green eyes crinkled at the corners.

She couldn't help smiling back, but she absolutely refused to think about the strange *squiggly* feeling she got deep inside when he smiled at her that way.

Josie Metcalfe lives in Cornwall with her long-suffering husband. They have four children. When she was an army brat, frequently on the move, books became the only friends that came with her wherever she went. Now that she writes them herself she is making new friends, and hates saying goodbye at the end of a book—but there are always more characters in her head, clamouring for attention until she can't wait to tell their stories.

Recent titles by the same author:

A WIFE FOR THE BABY DOCTOR
SHEIKH SURGEON CLAIMS HIS BRIDE*
THE DOCTOR'S BRIDE BY SUNRISE*
TWINS FOR A CHRISTMAS BRIDE
A MARRIAGE MEANT TO BE

Brides of Penhally Bay

A FAMILY FOR
HIS TINY TWINS

BY
JOSIE METCALFE

MILLS & BOON®

Pure reading pleasure™

First published in Great Britain 2009
Harlequin Mills & Boon Limited,
Eton House, 18-24 Paradise Road, Richmond, Surrey TW9 1SR

© Josie Metcalfe 2009

ISBN: 978 0 263 86835 7

Set in Times Roman 10½ on 12¾ pt
03-0409-49697

Printed and bound in Spain
by Litografia Rosés, S.A., Barcelona

A FAMILY FOR HIS TINY TWINS

CHAPTER ONE

HE WAS way beyond tired and should have been in bed and sound asleep hours ago, but the fear inside him wouldn't let Gideon close his eyes.

It was totally irrational, he knew, but somehow he was convinced that if he so much as took his eyes off those two tiny bodies for an instant, one or both of them would stop breathing.

'Twenty-six weeks!' he murmured in disbelief, shaking his head at how unbelievably tiny they were.

How could this have happened? The pregnancy had been progressing perfectly normally, as far as he had known.

Normally?

Ha! That was a joke.

Absolutely nothing about the existence of these babies had been normal, right from the first. And now there was the minute-by-minute danger that their tiny lungs would just be too underdeveloped to take the strain, or their hearts would fail, or, worst of all, they would suffer a catastrophic cranial bleed and never know the joys of a healthy normal life.

'Dr West?' said a quiet voice at his side, the soft hint

of an accent telling him that it was the nurse who'd been taking special care of his babies since they'd been brought into the unit. What was her name? Nadine? Natalie? No, Nadia. That was it—a name with a touch of the exotic, like her accent and the slight tilt to the corners of her eyes.

'Yes?' He glanced up into those soft hazel eyes, but quickly returned his gaze to watching the all but naked bodies sharing the isolette.

There was so much about them that reminded him of the utter vulnerability of baby birds, newly hatched from their shells, their skin so thin and so nearly transparent that he could swear that he could see every one of their veins through it.

'You need to take a break,' Nadia said, and he was almost amused by the edge of authority she tried to infuse into the words. It must be more difficult than usual for her to try to hand out orders when the person she was speaking to was a doctor in the same hospital, even though they didn't work in the same department.

'I'm all right,' he insisted, and realised that his voice sounded almost rusty from disuse. How long had he been sitting here, beside the clear plastic cot that held the fragile remnants of so many of his dreams?

'You are *not* all right,' she insisted in her turn. 'Dr West…' She paused with a huff of annoyance. 'What *is* your name? I cannot keep calling you Dr West every time I want to speak to you, not for all the months you are going to be visiting the unit.'

Months! He nearly groaned aloud.

The thought that this torment would last that long was too much to contemplate at the moment. It was almost a relief to be asked a question about something as ordinary as his name. Not that it was an ordinary name, thanks to his mother's sense of humour. While other parents chose to honour relatives or even geographical places with a namesake, he had been named after a certain book in the bedside drawer of the hotel where he'd been conceived.

'Gideon,' he said bluntly with a brief glance up at her delicate features just in time to see a swift frown pleat her forehead. 'But most people just call me Doc or West.'

'Gideon,' she repeated slowly, totally ignoring the alternatives he'd offered, and it was almost as if she were tasting the word…trying his name out in her mouth.

A totally inappropriate jab of awareness struck him, the first in such a long time that he couldn't remember when the last time had been. It had certainly been long before Norah had walked out on their marriage.

'I have never met anyone with this name before,' she said with a sudden smile. 'It's unusual…but strong. I like it.'

To his surprise, he found himself returning the smile, somehow feeling as if he'd just managed to reconnect with the world around him.

'Gideon, listen to me,' she said, her expression returning to the look of concern she'd been wearing earlier. 'You know that this situation isn't going to get better in one day, or even one week. Here, in this unit, is not like your department. In A and E you maybe see a patient for five minutes or, at most, a few hours before you send them home or admit them to one of the wards. Here, a patient can be with us for months, and the journey will be hard…very hard. So, it is important for the parents to take care of themselves properly so that *they* don't become sick, because, we need you to be strong enough to help us to take care of your babies.'

'So, if it's important for me to be here for the babies, why are you trying to make me leave?' He knew he was probably being argumentative for the sake of it, but that was what fear and exhaustion seemed to be doing to him…turning a normally rational man into one who picked a fight because of a totally irrational fear that his babies would die if he wasn't there.

'Because you need a break,' she said firmly, obviously having no intention of backing down. 'You need some food and to stretch your legs. And you need a shower and a change of clothes.'

That startled a brief burst of laughter out of him.

'I look and smell that bad?' he challenged, and was fascinated to see the swift wash of a blush sweep into her cheeks.

'I didn't mean to insult you,' she said hurriedly. 'I only—'

'It's too late to apologise now,' he said as he forced himself to straighten up out of the torture of the plastic chair. 'You've wounded my feelings. I shall go and find some clean clothes.'

'And don't come back until you've had some sleep, too,' she said as he started to make for the door of the unit, even as he tried to keep those two precious little bodies in sight right up to the last second.

'That will be the hardest part,' he admitted quietly, surprised to hear himself voicing his fears to someone who was little more than a complete stranger. 'I won't be able to sleep until I'm sure they're safe…that they're not going to die.'

'Then you are going to be one very tired man,' she pointed out. 'It could be weeks or even months before we can be certain of that.' But he somehow knew that she understood what he'd been saying and sympathised.

Nadia was relieved that the monitor attached to the smaller of her two new charges didn't go off until their father was out of earshot.

'Otherwise I would never have got him out of here, would I, little man?' she murmured as she swiftly checked each of the myriad leads that coiled away from the tiny bodies.

'Aha!' she exclaimed softly as she disentangled one of them from the grasp of a minute hand as gently as possible, always remembering that when they were this premature their skin was as fragile as wet tissue paper. 'So, little girl, you wanted to see how quickly I would react when you pulled your brother's sensor off, did you? Well, I spotted it right away, so you needn't think that I'm going to let you get away with that trick a second time.'

She applied a thin strip of adhesive tape to the offending monitor to make absolutely certain that it couldn't happen again when their father was there. Otherwise, as tightly wound as he was, she might end up having to resuscitate him.

'Not that it would be a hardship,' she whispered, more to herself this time. He was a good-looking man with his dark hair and startling green eyes, and when he'd smiled…

She shook her head sharply to banish such crazy

thoughts. Apart from the fact that he was a married man with two vulnerable babies, she wasn't interested in how good-looking any man was. She had barely survived her last encounter with one, and had no intention of risking that again any time soon.

That man had also been the reason she'd moved to a city as large as London and changed her name, hoping that she would never be found among so many millions.

In her own country, to have tried to earn her living in such a job as this would have made her easily traceable, especially for someone with Laszlo's connections. Here, because she'd been willing to study and work so hard, she'd been able to gain more and more qualifications. Now she'd achieved her dream and was looking after the tiniest patients imaginable, smaller even than her own daughter had been when she'd been born.

If she had been living here then, would little Anya have been saved? She smiled sadly at the pointless question because, of course, if she'd been living here, her daughter wouldn't have existed in the first place.

'So, now you are just a sad memory, my precious girl,' she whispered, heartbroken as ever by the fact that she didn't even have a photograph as a memento. 'And now I take care of other babies in your name so that their mothers and fathers will not know my heartache.'

'What do you find to talk about all day?' Staff Nurse Jenny Barber asked, her blue eyes as inquisitive as ever as she tried to come to grips with all the finer details of her new placement. 'Every time I look across at you, you're saying something to them. Do you really think they're listening?'

'I'm sure of it,' Nadia said with quiet certainty.

'There are few mothers who do not talk to their unborn child, and for many of those whose babies have to come here, it is impossible for them to be with their child all the time. So I talk to them so they will not forget that there is someone here who cares for them, even if my voice is not the one they are accustomed to.'

'You don't think that there's so much noise in here— with all the monitors and so on—that it's just one more sound to bombard them?'

'Not if I use the right tone to my words,' Nadia replied, as ever keeping that tone soft and gentle so that she didn't startle the babies with sharp or sudden noises. Their hearts were working hard enough already, without having to cope with sudden spikes as their systems were flooded with adrenaline with each shock.

'How are they doing?' asked Josh Weatherby, the unit's consultant, even before he'd finished scrubbing and gloving and tying on a disposable apron.

'Good, so far,' Nadia confirmed, and had to stifle a smile when she saw that his hair was ruffled and his shirt less than perfectly tidily tucked into the waistband of his suit trousers.

Obviously, something had finally happened between him and the newest doctor on the unit's team. And about time, too. It had been almost painful seeing the way he and Dani Dixon had been surreptitiously watching each other with longing in their eyes while trying to behave in a properly professional manner.

She stifled a brief pang of envy for their happiness, but she'd known for a long time that she would never experience such feelings for herself—her past had made certain of that.

'Hmm,' Josh murmured as he studied the latest figures and test results. 'These would definitely have been much better at twenty-six weeks gestation if they hadn't been twins. And we're going to have the usual problem stabilising their oxygen levels because there just wasn't enough time to get any steroids into the mother.'

'Have you heard how the mother is doing?' Nadia was always concerned about the women who developed eclampsia…not just because of their clinical condition but because it could sometimes be days before they could be stabilised enough to be able to see their babies for the first time. Inevitably, that could cause problems with bonding with their children.

'Not so good, immediately after the birth. For a while it looked as if they were going to have a serious problem with her blood pressure, because it stayed dangerously high. But it's started to come down now.'

It fascinated Nadia to watch the way he could hold a conversation without breaking his concentration on what he was doing to one of their patients. And, for a man, he had beautiful hands. Long-fingered, almost slender, but so deft and sure in everything they did.

She was surprised to realise that she'd noticed that Gideon West's hands were a similar sort of shape. Elegant and lightly tanned and with neatly trimmed, scrupulously clean nails, they were the sort of hands that would be a pleasure to watch, whatever they were doing, but especially when the time came to cradle one of his little babies.

'Is something wrong?' demanded a husky voice, and there was the man, in person.

Nadia turned and frowned when she saw him standing there, once more tying on a disposable apron.

He'd obviously showered and changed his clothes in the short time that he'd been away from the unit, and he'd even had a shave, but she doubted that he'd paused long enough to have anything to eat or drink and she didn't need to look at the shadows under his eyes to know that he definitely hadn't had any sleep.

'Nothing major to report,' Josh said easily as he straightened up from the cot, 'apart from all the usual complications from the fact that they've arrived too early.'

'And your wife's blood pressure has started to come down,' Nadia added cheerfully. 'Were you able to go in to see her after you'd had your shower?'

'She's not my wife,' Gideon said bluntly, and her shock at his apparently offhand manner must have shown on her face because he continued. 'She was a surrogate, paid to carry a child for my wife and me, and had absolutely no interest in the pregnancy other than as a means to make money.'

'But…' Nadia couldn't imagine any woman not becoming attached to the child she was carrying. She certainly hadn't been able to, even considering the circumstances of Anya's conception. 'I'm sorry. I shouldn't have assumed,' she said, not believing for a moment that he was as unfeeling as he was trying to appear and wondering why there had been no mention of his wife in all the hours that he'd spent beside their children. Surely she should be here, sharing his concern for the welfare of their new family.

'Well, whatever the circumstances, you don't need to worry about her,' Josh said with a reassuring smile in Gideon's direction. 'They're taking good care of her up in ICU, so you can concentrate on these two.

But don't forget to pace yourself, West. You need to get as much sleep as you can because you won't get much once you take the babies home, not for at least the first year.'

'If I ever get to take them home,' Gideon said as he gazed down at the frail little bodies curled up together in the single cot. 'When they look like this…so desperately vulnerable…it's hard to believe that they could ever survive.'

'We've brought smaller ones than this through,' Josh told him proudly. 'And Nadia is our most experienced nurse, so we're giving them the best possible chance.'

It was embarrassing to be spoken of in this way, but she doubted that Gideon had even heard what Josh had said, his whole concentration fixed on the strange jerky movements that one of the babies had started to make.

'What's happening? What's the matter with her?' he demanded sharply, and Nadia smiled reassuringly.

'Relax, Gideon,' she said gently, for the first time in her life struck by the urge to reach out to a man with a soothing hand. 'It's only an attack of hiccups,' she explained, and was delighted to hear that he was able to laugh at himself for panicking.

Later that day or possibly the next, Gideon wasn't sure—in fact, he couldn't remember when he'd last slept—having spent so many hours recently sitting in that uncomfortable plastic chair beside his babies' isolette, he opted to take the stairs down to A and E.

'Hey, West, how's it going? You look dreadful,' the junior registrar said by way of greeting when he pushed his way into the staff lounge.

'Thanks for that,' he said wryly. 'Just what I needed to hear.'

'Well, I'm sorry if the truth hurts,' John said unrepentantly. 'But how *are* things going upstairs? Are the babies holding their own?'

'How can anybody tell?' Gideon countered wearily. 'They're just so damn small, you can hardly see them for all the wires and tubes. And have you ever seen how tiny the disposable nappies are? Not even as long as my hand when they're completely opened out…too small for most dolls.'

'It's hard to imagine.' The younger man shook his head. 'So, how long do you think it'll be before you're back at work? Only I've got to tell you, we've been absolutely swamped and the department manager is running round like a headless chicken, shipping patients out right left and centre, regardless of whether we've finished stabilising them or treating them, just so we don't breach the government's guidelines for waiting times.'

'That's crazy!' Gideon exclaimed, almost relieved to have something else to focus on, even if it was hospital politics. 'It just doesn't make sense.'

'Neither does the fact that the bean-counters will be down on us like a ton of bricks if too many patients stay here even one minute longer than they should.' His colleague warmed to his theme. 'Do you know, I had an elderly lady with a broken hip in first thing this morning, and by the time I'd waited for the X-rays and blood tests and so on, her initial analgesia was wearing off and she needed an injection into the joint to make her comfortable before she was jostled all the way up to the ward to wait to go to Theatre.'

'And?' Gideon had a horrible feeling he knew where this was going.

'And, because she was getting close to breaching the waiting guidelines, she was whisked out of A and E and taken up to the ward where she had to wait in agony for another two hours before there was a doctor free to give her some pain relief. Now, you tell me how *that* sort of stupidity can be good for the patients?'

'That's even worse than having to take an ingrown toenail through for treatment ahead of a dislocated shoulder or a heart attack *just* because he's been waiting longest, not because he's the most urgent case medically,' Gideon said darkly. 'Politicians and bean-counters don't understand that these arbitrary time limits just *don't* work; they never will, especially when some patients need to stay with us *longer* than the guidelines allow for to be treated effectively.'

'Like that car-accident guy the other day,' John pointed out. 'By the time we'd X-rayed him, sorted out his fluids, ruled out internal injuries and stabilised his broken bones, we'd saved his life *but*, because we'd kept him down here for three minutes longer than we should, we got rapped over the knuckles. It's madness!'

'Unless you're the man with the ingrown toenail, when you're delighted to find that you take precedence over the heart-attack victim or the dislocation because *you've* been here longer and *he's* just arrived. It's enough to make you wonder why you bother doing the job sometimes.'

'But then you go upstairs and see what they can do for premature babies, and you know it's all worthwhile?' John suggested, knowing that Gideon would have to agree.

'Too true. But I honestly never thought about the complexity of what they have to do up there. And so much of it's on a minute-by-minute basis, checking blood gases, fluids in and out, temperature, blood pressure, pulse…it's just never-ending.'

'I must admit, my paeds experience during training involved rather older patients. I thought the really tiny ones just slept a lot and only needed attention when something went wrong, but that was before a family friend had a premature kid and told me all about it in exhaustive detail. I certainly wouldn't want the job,' the younger man admitted. 'At least, in A and E, we don't have to see anyone for more than four hours unless they're transferred next door to the observation ward.'

Gideon rubbed his hands over his face, afraid that he would soon reach the limits of his endurance, but until both babies were reasonably stable, he just didn't like leaving them.

'Anyway, you didn't answer my question,' John pointed out. 'When *will* you be back to take over your share of the load?'

'Not for a day or two yet,' he said bluntly, fighting back a feeling of panic at the mere thought of abandoning his babies for any length of time. 'I only came down to make my excuses in person and to grab some clean clothes from my locker.'

He hadn't left the hospital premises to go back to his flat since the babies had been born. It was only a ten-minute journey, but he was terrified that if he went that far away it would take too long to get to them if they had a sudden crisis. Even a trip to the cafeteria seemed too far and would take too long, so he'd been

existing on snacks from the nearest vending machine—
not the healthiest of diets, but he didn't care about that
at the moment. There would be plenty of time to get
his clothes and meals sorted out once the babies were
a bit stronger.

Mind you, he'd be surprised if Nadia didn't say
something to him before then. Each time she came back
on duty he see her looking him over with those intent
hazel eyes and was certain that she could tell just how
little food and rest he'd had.

At the thought of the disapproving way she would
press her lips together he actually found himself having
to suppress a smile.

She was such a quiet person and she actually said
more to the babies than she did to him, but Nadia
somehow managed to let him know exactly what she
thought of him and his obsessive need to be close to
those fragile little beings.

He ran his hands through his hair tiredly as he began
to make his way back up the interminable stairs. It had
been nearly two hours since he'd come down them, ex-
pecting his visit to A and E to take no longer than ten
minutes, but once his colleagues had realised he was
there, it was surprising that any patients had been seen
in the department as everyone had crowded around to
ask for a progress report.

'Have you got a photo?' one of the women had
demanded, and he'd reluctantly extracted it from his
wallet.

Nadia had arranged for the picture to be taken of the
babies on their first day in the unit, telling him that it was
the first of many that would chart their progress. But this

was the first one and therefore very precious, and it had felt strange to watch it being passed from hand to hand.

Now he was on his way back to his babies, feeling as if days rather than hours had passed since he'd been with them and filled with a rising sense of anxiety that something might have happened to them while he'd been away.

He took the final flight two stairs at a time and his heart was pounding when he tried to shoulder his way through the door to the unit, completely forgetting for a moment that it was a far more secure place than A and E.

His shoulder certainly didn't appreciate his lapse in concentration, and he didn't seem to be able to focus properly on the buttons he needed to press to gain entry to the unit.

Finally, he got it right and the lock clicked open so suddenly that he almost fell full length into the hallway, his feet apparently unable to obey the commands his brain was sending.

His knees weren't co-operating either, refusing to lock to keep him in an upright position... And now there was a strange rushing, roaring, echoing sound in his ears...and someone was turning the lights down in the corridor until they were so low that...that he couldn't really make out where he was supposed to be going or...or what he was supposed to be...

'You stupid man!' exclaimed a voice somewhere in the encroaching darkness right beside him. 'Get down before you fall down!'

The arm around his shoulders was surprisingly effective at supporting him as he was lowered to the floor, whether he wanted to submit or not. And he didn't.

'Stay where you are,' said the same bossy voice, sounding strangely like Nadia's, although he'd never heard her sound anything but softly spoken and gentle, even when she was remonstrating with him. 'You're not in a fit state to *sit* up, never mind *stand* up.'

'I need…I need to get to the nursery…to the babies…I need… They need—'

'They need a father with enough brains to look after himself, so he doesn't go passing out in the middle of the corridor,' interrupted the voice with a definite snap of anger. 'How long is it since you ate anything? When did you last sleep? Probably before the babies were born,' she said, answering her own question.

'I'll be all right,' he muttered defensively. 'I just need to spend time…I have to be there, in case—'

'Your babies have round-the-clock attention and supervision,' she interrupted again. 'You, on the other hand, need a nanny to tell you when to eat your food and when to go to bed.'

Josh didn't know whether to feel insulted at her assessment, or whether to wish there *was* some kindly person who could see him through the nightmare into which his life had been plunged.

'How are you feeling now?' she asked.

His head wasn't swimming as much, and his pulse had returned almost to normal, and apart from the fact that he was lying on the floor in front of who knew how many of his colleagues he was practically fine.

'Stupid,' he said succinctly, and forced himself to open his eyes to see just how many people were witness to his weakness.

The only eyes looking down at him were Nadia's hazel ones, and in spite of the impatience he'd heard so clearly in her voice, there was nothing other than concern in their expression.

'That would be logical,' she said dryly, and automatically reached out to offer him help to regain his feet.

He must have been feeling shakier than he would admit, even to himself, because he took hold of that slender hand with a feeling of relief.

The sharp shock of awareness as he wrapped his fingers around hers made him realise that this was the first time that they had ever touched without at least one layer of disposable glove between them. And the fact that she pulled her hand away as soon as he was upright and immediately plunged it into her tunic pocket told him that she'd been aware of the electric tingle between them, too.

'Where are you going?' he demanded when she took off along the corridor in the opposite direction from the nursery.

'To get you a drink and something to eat,' she said without the slightest trace of hesitation in her stride.

'But…what about the babies?' he demanded, the sense of urgency that had driven him to take the stairs two at a time returning to hit him like an avalanche. 'You should be with them. They shouldn't be left alone, not while they're so—'

'They are *not* alone,' she snapped crossly even as she straight-armed the staffroom door open. 'This is my break. Laura is looking after them for me.'

'But—'

'Get in here, Gideon, before I call Mr Weatherby and tell him to ban you from the unit,' she ordered, standing in the doorway while he hesitated in the middle of the corridor, torn.

'*Ban* me!' he exclaimed in disbelief. 'Why on earth would he do that? I'm their father. I've a *right* to be with them.'

'Unless you're judged to be a danger to them,' she pointed out with perfect resembleness. 'And I would say that falling over in a dead faint, with the potential for pulling out their monitor leads or disrupting their oxygen supply…or even tipping over their cot so that they fall on the floor on their heads…would definitely constitute a danger.'

'I did *not* fall over in a dead faint!' he exclaimed. 'I was just a bit…breathless after running up the stairs.'

'If that is what you want to tell yourself,' she said as she calmly took a plastic box out of the fridge. 'But I'd advise you to sit down before those shaky legs of yours dump you on the floor…again.'

His head still felt as if it was partly filled with cotton wool and she wasn't wrong about the shakiness of his legs, but it was mostly sheer fascination with this new side to her character that had him following her suggestion and choosing the end of the nearest couch to sit on.

Well, it was more as if he collapsed into the corner of the couch, the strength deserting his knees almost before he could get there.

'Here,' she said, and held a tall glass of water out to him. 'You're probably borderline dehydrated, on top of everything else. The temperature has to be kept

high for the babies, and you have to remember to com-
pensate for that.'

Gideon took one look at the slender hand holding out
the glass and the drops of water running down it to bead
on her soft flesh and suddenly realised just how badly
he needed a drink of something cold.

'Thanks,' he mumbled as he took it from her, this
time careful to avoid any physical contact between the
two of them.

It was nothing more than cold tap water but it felt so
good going down that it could have been some price-
less vintage.

'Take one,' she said as he lowered the empty glass,
and he saw that she was holding out a plastic box of
sandwiches.

'That's your lunch,' he objected when he saw that
the box was filled with obviously home-made trian-
gles of bread.

'There's plenty,' she said dismissively and, to his
surprise, she deposited the box on the seat beside him
and turned to deal with the boiling kettle. 'They're
chicken salad,' she said over her shoulder. 'I cooked the
chicken myself.'

They certainly smelled appetising, and before he
could allow his manners to deny him something that
looked so tasty, he reached into the box to take one out.

The first mouthful was enough to remind his body
that eating was something that had been virtually forgotten in the last few days.

'Oh!' he groaned as the flavours of that first sublime
mouthful mingled in his mouth. 'That is *so* good.'

The words must have been garbled around his hasty

second mouthful but her quick smile told him that she'd understood.

It also told him that she'd never actually smiled at him before, otherwise he would have realised, much sooner, just how beautiful she was.

CHAPTER TWO

NOT that he had any right to notice that she was beautiful, Gideon reminded himself sternly as he forced himself to focus on the sandwich. The only thing he should be concentrating on was the health and safety of those two tiny babies just along the corridor, so the quicker he finished eating the sooner he would be able to get back to them.

There was almost no conversation between the two of them as they made further inroads into the box of sandwiches.

Gideon knew that his silence was due to the fact that his appetite had just returned with a vengeance, but he had no idea why Nadia should suddenly be so tongue-tied. She certainly hadn't been shy about telling him what an idiot he'd been over the last couple of days.

In his own defence, he was overwhelmingly aware that he was the only person these two tiny babies had in the whole world, and his responsibility to be there for them, to protect them and make sure they were being treated properly, had become his most important duty.

'How have the babies been, the last couple of hours?' he asked, suddenly remembering just how long ago he'd left them to go down to A and E.

'Why do you do that?' Nadia asked.

'Do what?' He blinked, looking from the crumbs he was brushing from his trousered thigh with one hand to the mug of tea he'd been holding in the other, manfully trying to ignore the foul taste of all the sugar she'd stirred into it.

'You always call them "the babies",' she pointed out. 'Why have you not given them names yet?'

She certainly knew where to land the punches, even when she didn't know there were any targets to aim at.

'Because my wife and I never managed to agree on any names for the babies,' he told her.

Not that agreeing on something like baby names would have made any difference to the way their marriage had ended. When he'd looked back on it, he'd realised that, once she'd been told that she'd never be able to have a child of her own, she hadn't seen any point in being married to him any more. Unfortunately, they'd already embarked on the surrogacy route by the time she'd made her decision.

The ultimate irony had been that the very day that she'd served him with divorce papers, he'd received the phone call to inform him that the surrogate they'd chosen to carry a child for them was pregnant.

'What were *your* choices?' she asked with an encouraging smile. 'Something awful?'

'Amy and Adam,' he said, a little self-consciously. 'I didn't want to know the sex of the baby until it was born, so I chose a name for either eventuality. But that was before I knew there were going to be two of them.'

'And your wife?' Nadia prompted. 'What were her choices?'

'Zecharias and Zenobia,' he said with a grimace.

'Poor little babies!' she exclaimed, then covered her mouth with an apologetic hand. 'I'm sorry. That was rude! But they are such very *big* names for such tiny people. I think that Amy and Adam will be a much better fit. Do you think so?'

Now that he thought about it, he did think that his choices were the right ones for those little scraps of humanity, especially as he was going to be the one using them for however long his children managed to live.

'Yes, I *do* think so,' he said firmly, then announced, formally, 'Their names are Adam and Amy West.' And he was suddenly aware of a strange sensation as if a weight had been lifted off his shoulders.

'Good,' Nadia said, with a smile that lit her hazel eyes with hints of gold. She got to her feet and briskly brushed the front of her uniform tunic and gave the hem a swift tug, then took her mug across to rinse it out. 'Now, you sit there and finish your food and your tea,' she said.

Gideon blinked, suddenly realising that he had been sitting there following her every move as she smoothed her clothing over her slender hips and tidied away the remains of the lunch she'd shared with him so generously.

'I should go and see the babies...Adam and Amy,' he corrected himself swiftly when she frowned at him.

'You should sit here for a moment,' she countered. 'I don't want you collapsing all over my little patients.' She paused a moment beside him, and for a second every nerve stood to attention when he thought she was going to reach out and touch him.

'Gideon,' she said softly, twining her fingers together almost as if she was having to stop herself making contact, and for one crazy moment he almost wished that she would lose the fight. It seemed as if half a lifetime had passed since anyone had touched him with concern and he almost ached for the feeling that *someone* cared.

'You know that I would tell you immediately if there was something wrong with your babies?' she continued, snapping him out of his mental ramblings with a jerk. 'You know that you can trust me to look after Amy and Adam?'

He felt at a disadvantage sitting there, having to look up at her earnest expression and trying to read her honesty. He'd thought that he'd known the woman he'd married, that he could trust her. Otherwise he'd never have made her his wife. And look how that had turned out.

Could he trust his instincts when they were telling him that Nadia was very different, that she was someone he could trust with the lives of the only children he was likely to have?

'I'll sit here for a little while longer,' he conceded, common sense briefly overriding his obsessive need to be close to Adam and Amy. If he hadn't convinced himself that something would go wrong if he wasn't there with them, he probably wouldn't have hurried up the stairs like that and made a fool of himself by collapsing in front of Nadia.

'Finish your tea and relax,' she advised. 'We'll see you later.'

Against his will, Gideon found himself following her with his eyes as she left the room, and he couldn't help noticing how quietly she moved, with the elegant poise of a dancer.

Did she dance? he wondered idly as he let his head fall back. He could imagine that she would be good at it, her body lithe and fit and her height… He guessed she would be about half a head shorter than him, and if she was wearing heels, that would make her the perfect height, the perfect height for him to wrap his arms around, her legs the perfect length to mesh with his as they stepped rhythmically together and her mouth just perfect for him to tilt his head and share a kiss at the end of the dance…

Nadia pushed the door open a crack and gave a nod of satisfaction when she saw Gideon was still fast asleep.

The sign she'd stuck on the door—'Let sleeping doctors lie'—had made the rest of the staff smile, and they'd all been quite happy to share the spare kettle in Caitlin's office on a temporary basis.

She'd actually been surprised that her ploy had worked quite so well. She hadn't expected him to do much more than sit down for the length of time it took him to eat a final sandwich and finish his a mug of tea. The fact that he'd actually succumbed to his exhaustion and was still sleeping more than two hours later was more than she'd hoped for.

Perhaps, when he woke, he'd be more amenable to the idea of going home to sleep properly in his own bed and let his body return to a more normal existence.

'You may as well come in,' Gideon grumbled in a voice still husky with lingering sleep.

'You're awake!' she exclaimed, and realised that she wasn't certain whether she was disappointed that he hadn't slept longer or pleased that he was awake enough to speak to her.

'No thanks to you,' he pointed out with a scowl. 'What did you put in those sandwiches? Or was there something in the tea?'

'No! Nothing!' she exclaimed, stung that he would think her capable of drugging him. 'I would not do this to you, even though I knew you needed to sleep.'

'Hey! Calm down, Nadia, that was a joke,' he soothed, clearly surprised by her reaction. 'I fully realise that I was so tired that all it took was sitting down in a quiet place for me to fall asleep. What I don't understand is how you managed to keep everyone out of here long enough for it to happen.'

'That was easy,' she said, going back to reach out to peel the sign from the outside of the staffroom door and handing it to him. 'So, why did you wake up? I know that no one came in here, and the telephone was unplugged so it would not ring.'

'Ah, but you forgot about mobile phones,' he said, holding up the little gadget with a grimace. 'The human resources department has ways of tracking us down, especially when they want to inform us that we're not entitled to paid leave unless we prove that we've satisfied all the relevant criteria and filled in all the forms…in triplicate.'

'And what did you say to them?'

'Nothing repeatable, initially,' he admitted, and she could imagine that he wouldn't be the most even-tempered of people when he came up against mindless bureaucracy, especially if he was woken from a sound sleep. 'Then I told them that I was spending time with my children while they're in Intensive Care.'

'And?' She knew from his expression that there was

more, and wondered when she'd begun to be able to read him in this way. She didn't usually allow anybody close enough to form that sort of bond.

'And they informed me that it was fraud to claim time off to be with non-existent children, because they had no record that I have any children, just a wife.'

'And you told them…?' She perched on the arm of the nearest chair, actually finding that she was enjoying listening to his account, fascinated to see yet another side of the man.

'I told them that it was time that somebody in their department actually *earned* the salary they were being paid, and updated their records with the information they'd been given—firstly, that I've been divorced for several months and, secondly, that I am now the father of two babies currently residing in an incubator in this hospital.'

'And so you were woken from the first sleep you have had in too many days by someone wasting your time,' she said crossly.

'That seems to be what you get when the hospital is staffed by more administrative staff than doctors and nurses added together,' he grumbled. 'You know, we were actually allocated several extra nurses on A and E, to speed up the treatment of the more minor cases and free up the senior staff to deal with the more serious injuries and illnesses. But by the time they'd appointed someone to check up to see whether the hospital was getting value for money out of the new staff, and that they were actually speeding up the treatment of patients, and then appointed someone to work as their secretary, and someone to collate all the statistics and someone to go to the meetings to report back to the next level of bean-counter, and so on and so on, they'd actually spent all the money that should have gone to pay the nurses' salaries and had to sack the nurses in order to save the money to streamline the operation of A and E. But, of course, all the new administrative staff kept their jobs!'

'You are joking!' Nadia knew that bureaucratic inter- ference in the day-to-day and minute-to-minute running of hospitals was actually causing more problems than it was solving, but she hadn't realised that things had become this chaotic.

'Not by much,' Gideon said darkly. 'I'm more and more convinced that they could sack fifty per cent of the administrative staff and the only difference it would make to the running of the hospital would be that there would be less paperwork and more time to treat patients… Oh, and we'd have all the money we could ever want to employ all the doctors and nurses we needed.'

'And yet, as bad as it gets, you would not change your profession,' she said, not even needing to make it a question. She already knew that he was the sort of person to whom dedication to duty would be paramount.

'You're right,' he admitted. 'Being a doctor is all I've ever wanted to do, but…' He sighed.

'But?' she prompted.

'But I have to admit that the stupidity of the current system, where watching the clock matters more than treating our patients the way they need to be treated, is really getting me down.'

'Do you see any way of changing things to make them better?' Her memories of the system in her own country were so harrowing that, as bad as it could be here, it would always be better than what she'd come from.

'Honestly? No,' he said shortly. 'Not unless the hospitals can escape from the stranglehold of the politicians, and as I can't see that happening any time soon, I must admit I've seriously thought about joining the thousands of doctors and nurses who've emigrated to somewhere they're valued properly…like Australia, for example.'

He yawned widely, then apologised. 'I'm sorry, but I tend to get very grumpy when I'm tired.'

'And, as you're a doctor, you're tired most of the time, so that means…' She left the logical end of the sentence open, surprised that she'd actually dared to tease him but delighted when he laughed aloud at the inference.

'So you think I'm grumpy all the time?' he challenged.

'Not all the time,' she corrected him seriously. 'Only when you're tired.'

'And getting woken up like that by HR didn't help. How long was I asleep? Ten minutes?'

'More than two hours,' Nadia corrected him, and nearly laughed aloud at his look of shock.

'Two hours!' he exclaimed in disbelief. 'And you're in here… What's happened? Something's happened to the babies…to Adam and Amy.'

'Nothing's happened,' she said soothingly, but she should have known that mere words wouldn't convince him. He was halfway to the door already. 'Gideon, please. Calm down,' she pleaded, and grabbed his arm as he strode past her.

He stopped as suddenly as if he'd walked into a brick wall and she only realised what she'd done when she saw that he was staring at the place where her hand touched the naked skin of his arm.

It felt hot, or was it her hand that felt hot against him, hot enough to sizzle, almost as if there was an electric charge between them?

'Sorry,' she muttered, and snatched her hand away, rubbing her palm against her tunic to try to dispel the strange lingering sensation. 'I just wanted to reassure you that your babies are fine, that they're asleep and their oxygen sats have remained within acceptable limits for nearly six hours now.'

He looked almost as shaken as she felt and those stunning green eyes that were usually so clear had a slightly bewildered expression in them.

'They're asleep?' She saw the tension slowly seep out of his shoulders then drain out of his face, leaving him looking more tired than ever.

'Peacefully.' She nodded. 'And that's what you should be doing, properly in your own home.'

'I know, but…' He shook his head and she could imagine how torn he was feeling…how desperate *she* would be feeling if they were *her* babies and she was being told to go away and leave them without her. It was bad enough having to switch off her protective instincts at the end of her shift when they *weren't* her own.

'How far away from the hospital do you live?' she asked as an idea started to form in her head. 'More than half an hour?'

'Ten minutes…less if I run,' he corrected her. 'Why?'

'And I already know that you have a mobile phone otherwise you would still be asleep now,' she continued. 'So, if you were to give me your number, and I were to promise that I will phone you if there is a problem with Amy or Adam…?'

She could see that he was weighing up her offer, and crossed her fingers in the secrecy of her pocket that he would agree to the suggestion, for the sake of his own health.

'You would promise?' he asked, those beautiful eyes darkly serious.

'I would promise,' she repeated solemnly, then waited for his decision.

Knowing how desperately he'd fought to stay awake to be with his tiny son and daughter, she was touched beyond measure when he said softly, 'All right. I'll trust you,' and began to hunt for a pen to write his phone number down.

'Promise me you will get some sleep,' she said as she took the piece of paper from him, careful not to let their fingers touch and hoping he didn't notice her caution.

'All I can promise is that I'll try.'

Sleep was a long time coming, in spite of the fact that Gideon was totally exhausted.

Part of the problem was that his brain just wouldn't slow down, endlessly replaying the events that had led up to his current situation.

Not that he needed to relive the demise of his ill-fated marriage. That had been painful enough the first time around, with Norah's increasing desperation to have a child completely overshadowing all the good parts of their relationship. When even IVF hadn't worked, the realisation that she would never be able to conceive or carry a child of her own had been a bitter blow, especially to someone who had waited eagerly all her life to become a mother.

He'd understood her reluctance to adopt a child that bore no blood relationship to either of them, even though he didn't share her concern to the same extent, and when she'd decided that surrogacy had been the way she wanted to go, he'd been quite happy to agree if it would give her the family she wanted so desperately.

Unfortunately, he hadn't realised just how bad her depression had become after that final diagnosis had destroyed the last of her hopes.

By the time they'd contacted various agencies and begun the process that would hopefully result in a successful pregnancy, not only had she changed her mind about the surrogacy but she'd also decided she no longer wanted to be married to him.

He didn't think he'd ever forget the irony of opening an envelope containing the divorce papers while answering the phone to be told that the surrogate mother's pregnancy test had come back positive. But even that news hadn't changed Norah's mind.

The discovery, at the twelve-week scan, that there were *two* babies had filled him with a dizzying mixture of elation and terror.

The fact that multiple pregnancies carried far greater risks for mother and children was his initial concern, as were the logistics of bringing up twins as a single father working long hours in the stressful world of A and E. But as far as he was concerned, that was easily balanced by the joy that flooded through him at the thought that he would have *two* babies to shower all his love on, *two* babies who would give him cuddles and smiles.

To the surrogate mother, the news had been nothing more than a reason to double the amount of money she'd demanded for her services, and he'd been completely unsurprised to learn that once she was out of danger she hadn't once asked about the fate of the children she'd sheltered inside her body, even though half of every cell in their bodies contained her genes.

'You're on your own, mate,' he announced to the four walls of his bedroom, deliberately saying the words aloud. 'If those two little scraps ever survive the next few weeks, you're going to be all they've got in the world.'

And that certainly hadn't been his intention when he'd embarked on the process.

Having been shuffled around the fostering system for most of his childhood, he'd always believed that children deserved two parents to give them the security they needed. Of course, there were thousands of single parents who did a magnificent job of raising their children, but he'd always thought that any children he fathered would be within the bounds of a traditional two-parent family.

For Adam and Amy that wasn't going to happen. In fact, with a total lack of female relatives—of relatives of either gender, as far as he knew—it looked as if the closest the pair of them was going to get to being mothered was during their time in the unit, with Nadia and the other dedicated staff taking care of them so carefully.

Nadia.

Just thinking about her was enough to bring a smile to his face.

She'd seemed such a quiet and unassuming person when he'd first met her…but, then, he *had* been in shock with the premature delivery of the twins and not taking much notice of anything beyond their scrawny little bodies.

Well, she certainly hadn't been quiet and unassuming today.

He chuckled aloud at the way she'd torn a strip off him when he'd nearly passed out at her feet. And not all those words had been in English, so heaven only knew how salty her language might have been if he'd understood all of it.

She'd been devious, too, sitting him down in a reasonably comfortable chair with something to eat and a warm drink, knowing that his exhaustion would make him predisposed to sleep. If it hadn't been for that call from Human Resources, he might still be sleeping there, watched over by the same fiery little dragon who was taking care of his babies.

He remembered the way those hazel eyes of hers had lightened, glimmering with shards of gold when he'd made her laugh, and was surprised to feel the same tingle of electricity shimmering through him that he'd noticed when she'd put her hand on his arm.

'Strange,' he whispered, wondering sleepily whether it was something to do with static electricity. It certainly wasn't something he'd noticed before when he'd been in the unit. But, then, he hadn't touched her before… not skin to skin…

Skin to skin…? That was the wrong thought to have when he was trying to get to sleep, especially when he could all too easily picture the creamy perfection of her slender arms and her flawlessly symmetrical face. It was too easy to imagine what her willowy body would look like without the concealing tunic and trousers…to picture the way she would turn to him with that smile she always bestowed on his babies…to feel the gentle touch of her hands on *his* body even as he was exploring hers…

'Damn!'

Gideon swore as the strident sound of his phone dragged him out of one of the most sexually explicit dreams he'd ever had. He didn't think he'd been this aroused since…since making love had become nothing more than a means of trying to give Norah the baby she'd wanted.

'West,' he growled, his voice rusty with sleep and thick with arousal.

'Gideon? This is Nadia,' said the voice on the other end of the line, but it sounded very different from the way it had sounded in his dream.

Suddenly, the significance of hearing that voice doused any lingering arousal better than a bucket of cold water.

'What's the matter? What's happened to the babies?' he demanded, already on his feet and trying to dress one-handed.

CHAPTER THREE

'CALM down, Gideon,' Nadia said firmly, her accent somehow more noticeable on the phone...or had he just become accustomed to it in person?

'Don't tell me to calm down,' he snapped as he hopped on one foot, trying to get the other one into his jeans, then immediately felt ashamed of himself for taking his bad temper out on her. It wasn't Nadia's fault that he'd been having an erotic dream about her. 'You wouldn't have phoned me if something wasn't wrong, so just tell me what it is.'

'Adam's temperature has gone up,' she said baldly, and the impact of the news was like a blow to his chest.

'What else?' he demanded, his brain already running through all the possible reasons why his son's temperature had risen.

'It might be that he's developing a respiratory problem...perhaps an infection?'

Gideon felt ill at the thought of that fragile body having to fight off an infection on top of struggling for life.

He was still tugging a thick sweatshirt over his head as he scooped his keys off the hall table. 'I'll be there in five minutes,' he said, even as he sent up a prayer that the roads would be relatively clear at this time of night. If the worst came to the worst, he didn't want to be stuck in traffic when his son's life was being overwhelmed by something as simple as a bacterial infection.

'I knew I shouldn't have listened to her,' he snarled viciously as he put the flat of his hand on the horn and blasted his way past another motorist dithering at a junction as the lights changed. 'I should have stayed with them.'

As if that would have made any difference to what Adam was going through, he admitted more sanely as he took the stairs up to the unit, not knowing whether it was the dread of what he was going to find or the memory of almost passing out that made him take them at a more sensible pace than last time.

'How is he?' he demanded from behind the mask he was donning as he joined the knot of people around the cot.

'Struggling,' Josh admitted sombrely as he looped the stethoscope over his head to dangle down either side of his chest.

'And Amy?' The two babies almost seemed to be holding on to each other and had never reminded him more of fledgling birds in a nest.

'She seems to be unaffected so far, but—'

'She's unaffected, but she's still sharing the cot?' Gideon interrupted heatedly. 'Are you *trying* to infect her, too?'

'*But,*' Josh repeated patiently, almost as if he was deliberately ignoring Gideon's charge, 'when we tried to take Amy away, to leave Adam isolated, they both became so distressed that we had to put her back in.'

'What?' Gideon couldn't believe what he was hearing. The babies were far too young to be able to express anything so sophisticated as loneliness...weren't they?

'It is true, Gideon,' Nadia said earnestly, carefully holding her hands away from him as she stepped closer, then seeming to make a deliberate decision to contaminate her gloves as she rested her hands on his clenched fists. 'The monitors went crazy on both of them, but especially on Amy. Her pulse and respiration went way up and her movements clearly showed that she was agitated. It was only when we put them back together that things calmed down again. And look,' she said with a nod in their direction, 'it's almost as if they're holding on to each other, as if to tell us to leave them alone.'

That was exactly the impression he'd had when he'd first caught sight of them, Gideon remembered, and the description was uncannily accurate. It *was* almost as if Amy was putting a protective arm around her little brother.

'So, what happens now?' Gideon asked wearily, wondering if this was the point when he had to resign himself to losing both of them. Biology being what it was, he'd actually allowed himself to hope that Amy might survive, even though her weaker male twin probably wouldn't. But in spite of the fact that she'd been born marginally the stronger of the two, she was still far too small to need the added strain of fighting off the infection if she caught it from Adam. 'What can we do to help them?

'You sit with them, and talk to them, and pray and hope,' Nadia said simply. 'And we will continue to do everything we can to support their immature immune systems so they can combat the infection.'

* * *

'Gideon, did you get any sleep at all?' Nadia asked when, finally, there were just the two of them left by the cot.

'Some,' he said, and was surprised to feel the beginnings of a blush heating his face when he remembered what had been going on inside his head while he'd been sleeping.

He knew he had absolutely no control over the dreams that came to him, but that didn't stop him feeling uncomfortable about talking to the woman who'd starred in them.

'You really need to go back home and get some more,' she advised gently. 'You look even worse than when you left the department earlier.'

'And you think I would be able to sleep, knowing what's going on in that cot?' he demanded, suddenly weary beyond belief.

'I know you won't,' she admitted. 'Not unless someone uses a…' she mimed swinging something at his head while she apparently searched for the word she wanted '…*cosh* on you.' She shook her head. 'If I hadn't promised that I would telephone you…'

'I'm glad you kept your word,' he said seriously. 'Now I know that I can trust you…' He glanced up at the big clock on the wall in the outer corridor, clearly visible through the glass wall of the nursery, and sighed heavily, torn by his body's need for rest and his heart's need to be here for his son.

'Will you try to sleep?' she asked. 'If you don't want to leave the hospital again, is there somewhere you could put your head down for a few hours?'

'I can't use the on-call bed in A and E, in case there's

a lull and the poor blighter on duty gets the chance to shut his eyes. No, I'll just stick it out until Adam's stable again.'

'Unless you stretch out on the couch in the staff-room,' Nadia suggested, then hurried on when he frowned. 'I know it's not ideal, but I'm sure that the other people who work on this unit would understand. They won't mind going on the tips of their toes around you.'

On the tips of their toes…Gideon found himself smiling as he replayed the slightly awkward phrase that Nadia had used and wondered just how long she'd been living in England. It was just the occasional trip in her grammar and that exotic lilt to her accent that gave her away and made him speculate just what had brought her here.

Had she done her nursing training in her own country and travelled abroad to gain greater experience?

Perhaps her homeland was one of the countries that paid their nurses less than they could earn in the British system, and it was the money that had drawn her? Although, having watched her dedication to her little charges, he seriously doubted that financial gain had been her motivation.

Did she have family who were relying on her to send back a slice of her wages to help them, he speculated, or was she, like him, essentially alone in the world?

Gideon's eyes popped open when he realised exactly what he was doing.

He *never* bothered to think about other people's private lives. In fact, that was one of the things that Norah had thrown at him when she'd said she was leaving him—the fact that he was far too self-contained.

Well, perhaps after a lifetime of never feeling that he belonged anywhere, he *had* been. He certainly hadn't been as devastated by her departure as his colleagues seemed to think he should be.

So, was he different now?

Perhaps the birth of Adam and Amy had brought about some strange fundamental change in him that had him wanting to know more about the people around him.

Or perhaps it was just that there was something about Nadia that had caught his attention and had him imagining the two of them exchanging the sort of basic information that had never really interested him before.

And why had that happened now…with her? She certainly hadn't given him the slightest indication that she would be willing to share such information. In fact, she must be the least inquisitive woman he'd ever met.

And the most self-contained, now that he thought about it. He knew almost nothing more about her than her name, and that had been given to him by someone else.

He shifted his position, trying vainly to find a comfortable place to put his shoulder without jamming his head under the wooden arm of the settee or having his legs hanging over the opposite end. This piece of furniture definitely wasn't made for someone more than five and a half feet tall at the most, and he was at least a head taller than that.

If he were asleep, perhaps he wouldn't notice the discomfort…at least, until he woke up with a stiff neck and a wrecked back…but while his thoughts were veering from worrying about Adam and Amy to wondering about Nadia, there was very little chance of dropping off.

Perhaps if he thought of a few questions to ask her, he'd have more luck, such as…where do you come from? And… What made you decide to come to England? And… Are you going out with anyone at the moment?

Whoa! Gideon brought his meandering thoughts to a screeching halt. Where had that last question come from?

He had absolutely no interest in the status of her private life because his own was non-existent, and would remain that way until those tiny babies were at least eighteen years old.

And now he was lying to himself, he admitted on a silent groan, knowing that there was no way he could switch off his unexpected attraction towards the intriguing woman caring for his babies…even though the fact of those babies' existence should come between himself and any thoughts of a relationship with a woman.

Realistically, he knew that, at the very best, he was in for several months of alternating crises and triumphs as Adam and Amy fought their way towards an existence independent of high-tech help. At worst, he could be looking at watching those two precious babies failing in that struggle, and mourning when they finally gave up the fight.

Whichever path they were destined to travel, he knew from his own work in the same hospital that the patients and their families had a strange love-hate relationship with the professionals who were treating them. Illogical as it was, he knew just how often he'd been vilified when he'd been unable to give a patient another chance at life.

He liked to think that, having been the victim of it himself, he would know better than to blame Nadia if the unthinkable happened and one or both of the babies didn't survive. But what if she were to suffer from that other curse of the medical profession…the unreasonable guilt that they hadn't been able to do more for their patient, that they hadn't been able to 'save' them?

His rusty chuckle startled him in the silence of the night when he realised that not only was he fantasising about a relationship with the woman, he'd also forecast the disastrous end of it, filled with recriminations when his babies didn't survive.

'But they *are* going to survive,' he declared firmly, needing to hear the words spoken aloud. 'Adam will battle off this infection, and the two of them will fight and develop and grow until they're strong enough to leave the hospital and start the rest of their lives.'

'Come on, my little rabbits,' Nadia crooned as she changed first one and then the other tiny disposable nappy.

She'd done this task so many thousands of times in her career that the process was completely automatic, but she still marvelled at how very fine a premature baby's skin could be; still had to be so very careful that she didn't scratch or abrade it, leaving a wound through which an infection could gain entry.

'Together we can take care of everything,' she murmured, unconcerned whether her words emerged in her first or her second language. The babies wouldn't care. They would respond to the tone of her voice rather than what she was saying. 'Together, we can do it. Together, we can make sure that you both grow big and strong, so you can go home with your daddy.'

She checked the positioning of each of the monitors

and the fine plastic tubes that conveyed the various fluids in and out of their bodies.

'Hopefully, it won't be long before you don't need help with your breathing, then we'll be able to hear your voices properly. Then you'll be able to shout to tell us when you're hungry,' she promised. 'Maybe, by then, we'll have found out whether the two of you have inherited your daddy's gorgeous green eyes and—'

A soft sound behind her had her glancing over her shoulder straight into the eyes in question, currently sporting a definite gleam of amusement.

'*Gorgeous green eyes?*' he repeated, teasingly, and she felt a wash of heat sweep up from her throat and into her face.

Why couldn't she have been using her own language when she'd said that, she mourned, or at least have finished talking to his babies before he came close enough to hear what she was saying?

'I…' She had to stop to clear her throat, her brain frantically searching for something to say that would minimise the embarrassment of the situation—although *he* didn't seem in the least bit embarrassed. In fact, he seemed almost pleased to have heard her admiring words. 'I always talk nonsense to the babies when I'm doing things to them, so I don't give them a shock when I touch them.'

His raised eyebrow told her he didn't buy her gabbled excuse, but he was enough of a gentleman not to challenge her on it. Or perhaps it was that he had more important things on his mind.

'How is Adam?' he demanded, already reaching for his son's file. 'Are the antibiotics working? Is his breathing easier? Is his temperature down? Has Amy caught it from him—whatever it is—or is she still all right?'

Nadia paused a second to absorb the avalanche of questions before she replied in the same staccato way.

'Better. Apparently. Yes. Yes. No, and yes.'

For several seconds she had the pleasure of knowing that she'd rendered him speechless, then he laughed and those gorgeous green eyes crinkled at the corners and it was her turn to have difficulty finding her tongue.

'OK. I deserved that,' he conceded. 'But I would be grateful for a *little* more detail.'

She couldn't help smiling back, or the feeling of amazement that trickled through her when she realised that she'd actually dared to tease a man for the first time. But she absolutely refused to think about the strange *squiggly* feeling that she got deep inside when he smiled at her that way.

'Adam seems to be doing a little better,' she told him, hoping that he couldn't hear in her voice that her pulse was racing in her throat. Was it actually due to excitement this time, rather than the dread to which she'd grown so accustomed? 'The antibiotics appear to be working because his temperature has come down a little and his breathing is marginally easier. And, so far, it seems as if Amy is still clear and unaffected by the bug.'

She saw his shoulders slump in evident relief and realised that this was a father who really cared about his babies. His insistence on spending so much time with them certainly wasn't just for show…to prove to his hospital colleagues his credentials as a concerned parent.

Although why she should have doubted him, she had no idea. Except in moments of extreme stress he'd never been anything less than courteous towards her or any of the other staff, and as for the way he'd hovered over those two tiny creatures, driving himself way beyond exhaustion…that should have been proof enough that he was nothing like Lasz—

No! Not him! She wouldn't…*couldn't*…even put the two men in the same thought. They were so completely opposite in every way that it was hard to believe that they could even exist on the same planet.

Her hands froze in mid-air as that thought ballooned inside her head, overwhelming in its significance.

Yes, Gideon *was* totally different from Laszlo, even though he shared the same basic genetic make-up of the other half of the human race. Even after all she'd gone through and her determination that she'd never risk getting into the same situation again, she knew without a shadow of a doubt that Gideon was someone of whom she need never feel afraid.

But what did that mean?

Was it just that he was a very rare…even unique… man, one who didn't feel the need to demonstrate his superiority over any female with the rough end of his tongue or his fists?

She shuddered at the memories that she was never quite able to banish and tried to focus, instead, on the fact that she was here, in London, working in a hospital where her hard-earned skills were valued every day by her colleagues and each of the tiny babies she tried to nurture into healthy life.

Every time she waved a family off as they took their precious baby home for the first time, Nadia felt a deep sense of satisfaction for a job well done, but sometimes, in the dark of the night, she wondered if she would ever feel completely fulfilled by what she did.

Her greatest fear was that only carrying a baby of her own would do that, in which case she was doomed for ever to remain unsatisfied because there was no chance that she would ever become pregnant again.

So, she would just have to take her pleasure in touching and holding each new charge put into her care, letting herself fall just a little in love with them and having another little piece of her heart broken as they left her to go home with their parents.

Occasionally, she would feel the claws of jealousy rip into her when she knew that she would be able to take care of these precious beings far better than their own mothers would; that she had so much love to give that she could probably even love them more, but that would never happen. She would always be the one left with a wistful smile on her face when the doors closed behind them, the smile fading as she turned to begin the essential rigorous cleaning of everything in the bay before her next little charge arrived.

'Are you all right, Nadia?' asked a husky voice, and she blinked, horrified to realise that she had no idea how long her thoughts had been rambling while Gideon had been sitting there beside the cot.

'Pardon?' she said, stalling for time. Had he been speaking to her, asking her questions? It was unforgivable that her concentration should have been so distracted, for even a moment. What if something had happened to Amy or Adam and she'd been so wrapped up in her thoughts that she hadn't noticed?

A monitor shrilled in the bay behind her and a nurse

scurried over to it, and she realised *that* could never happen. The sensors were set so finely that sometimes they seemed to go off for no reason at all, and there was no way she could *ever* ignore one of them.

'I wondered if you're all right,' he said, and she was surprised by his obvious concern for her. She knew he watched every little thing that happened with the babies but this was the first time that she'd realised that he might be keeping an eye on her, too. 'You seem a little…subdued this morning.'

'Probably. I'm just a little tired,' she said by way of excusing her inattention. 'It has been a long, stressful night and it is nearly the end of my shift.' As if that would make her brain switch off to Amy's and Adam's condition. She probably worried more about them when she was away from them than when she was here and able to do something for them.

'Do you live far away?' he asked, startling her with the personal question.

'Not far,' she said with an evasiveness that had quickly become second nature to her once she'd realised she was going to have to rely on her own efforts to escape Laszlo for good.

'Walking distance or have you got a car?' he prompted.

'Why?' The defensive question popped out before she could soften its bluntness.

'Just that the area around the hospital isn't the safest place for a woman to be alone at this time of the morning,' he said easily. 'If you were walking, I was going to offer you a lift, especially as it was starting to rain quite heavily as I arrived and the forecast doesn't speak of it getting any better all day.'

'Oh.' Surprise made her all but speechless. She could hardly remember the last time anyone had shown her such consideration. Still, her wariness was too ingrained for her to willingly let anyone know where she was living. 'Thank you, but it's only around the corner and it's probably quicker to walk there than go by car, especially with the one-way system.'

He must have read something of the tamped-down fear in her eyes or on her face because there was definitely a new watchfulness to the way he was looking at her.

Not that anyone else would have noticed it, unless they'd been spending as much time in his company as she had. His attentiveness towards Amy and Adam was every bit as intense, and his delight when she asked him to hold his son for a moment while she changed the bedding in the cot was almost incandescent.

'Hey, little man,' Gideon murmured softly to the little scrap of humanity that was barely longer than his hand. 'This isn't quite the way I thought I'd hold you for the first time, but…'

Nadia heard his voice grow thick as the emotions of the moment closed his throat, and she was hard-pressed not to cry herself. Only the fact that she was juggling the handful of tubes and wires attached to Amy gave her something to concentrate on to keep her composure. Still, her heart swelled with sympathy, and her respect for a man who clearly didn't care who saw the emotional tears slipping down his cheeks grew by the minute.

Gideon didn't think he'd ever forget the moment that Nadia placed Adam in his hands.

He was so tiny as to be almost weightless, a collection of desperately fragile bones covered in the thinnest of tissue-paper skin, but there, in that little chest, was a heart smaller than a walnut that was beating fast and furious in his determination to live.

And that *was* what it felt like.

Adam was so small and there were so many reasons why he shouldn't be alive, having been born this premature, but there, sprawled in his hands, Gideon was convinced he could feel that his son had no intention of doing anything but survive.

It wasn't until Adam had been returned to his cosy temporary home and had settled down peacefully again beside his sister that Gideon realised that his face was wet with tears he hadn't even been aware of shedding.

For just a second he'd been startled to realise that he'd lost control like that, then decided that he really couldn't care less if anyone else had been aware that he was crying. If the first moment a man held his son wasn't a time for emotions to overflow, then what was?

And, anyway, he rationalised as he surreptitiously mopped up the evidence, this room must have seen more than one person cry since the unit had opened. These walls must have contained more than their fair share of heartbreak along with the uplifting successes along the way.

A quick glance at Nadia told him that she was fully occupied with resetting the monitors after the babies' brief excursion out of their humidicrib, but he didn't doubt for a moment that she'd noticed his tears.

Did she think any less of him for his loss of control? He was unlikely to ever know. She was such a self-contained person that it was difficult to tell how she felt about anything…except the babies. It would only take a second for a complete stranger to know how she felt about them.

It was strange, now that he thought about it. There was a different person caring for the twins at each shift change, but in his mind it was Nadia he saw as their carer.

Was that because she genuinely seemed to care about them—monitoring their every hiccup and the minutest progress they made—as if they really mattered to her?

Not that the other specialist nurses didn't give them every bit as much attention when it was their turn, but somehow it was almost as if Nadia saw them as *her* babies, and consequently watched over them with the vigilance of a mother lion.

It felt good to know that someone besides him cared what happened to them, especially as it was obvious that the woman who had carried them all those months clearly didn't give a fig.

He'd actually made a special trip up to the ward to tell Fiona how the babies were doing and had been shocked by her callous dismissiveness.

Of course, he'd tried to convince himself that that it could be the woman's way of coping with the emotional wrench of giving away her babies, but somehow he doubted it. After all, her first reaction to learning that she was carrying two foetuses hadn't been the usual delight at the news of one of nature's magical surprises, but to immediately demand double the agreed fee, with a bonus if both survived.

No, she certainly didn't care about the babies the way Nadia did, and it had been clear from Fiona's parting words and the way she'd turned her back on him that her only concern was that she might not be able to collect that bonus.

'Please, Gideon.' Nadia's soft voice broke into his musings. 'Promise me that you will sleep.'

He blinked up into eyes filled with concern and for just one crazy moment his heart gave an extra beat at the thought that she really cared about him, too.

'I will not be able to rest if I am worrying about you as well as the babies. You need to be strong for them, not collapsing over them when they need you the most,' she continued, and he suppressed a wry smile. He should have known that her focus would be entirely on those precious babies. That was the way Nadia was.

Except…his logical mind added as he vainly tried to court sleep in the corner of the staffroom settee a few minutes later. Except it had felt as if there *had* been something personal in the way she'd pinned him down to that promise, and there had definitely been something…some awareness between them in the way neither of them could touch each other without feeling the jolt of a current of electricity at the contact. And he knew that she was feeling it, too, by the way she so carefully avoided touching him.

Was that where her wariness had come from when he'd tried to offer to see her safely home? Obviously, some caution was sensible when dealing with strangers, but he felt there had been a definite edge to her caginess about letting him know where she lived.

'Or perhaps she just thought you were being inappropriately nosy,' he muttered, and felt the tips of his ears burn with a blush at the possibility that she might believe he was trying to inveigle himself into her private life.

Where *had* that question come from this morning, asking her where she lived, for heaven's sake? It was none of his business where she lived, or with whom, even if he did find himself worrying about her safety as she made her way through the early-morning city streets.

CHAPTER FOUR

'AREN'T you glad to be back in A and E?' John taunted him as Gideon stripped off his vomit-stained scrubs with a grimace and threw them in the laundry bin.

'Overjoyed,' Gideon agreed as he grabbed a towel and stepped towards the shower cubicle. 'Drunken louts spoiling for a fight while I try to stitch their stupid heads are my favourite patients.'

He could hear his colleague's laughter over the sound of the pounding water, but concentrated instead on the pleasure of ridding himself of the garments decorated with second-hand beer and some lurid-coloured take-away meal and letting the hot deluge take the sour stench away.

Down here felt like another world when he compared it to the relatively calm oasis of the unit upstairs. Was it just because many of the tiny patients up there at the moment were on ventilators and were largely unable to voice their dissatisfaction at what was being done for them? That certainly wasn't the case down in A and E. Even when the staff here were doing their absolute best for the patients, the thanks and praise were thin on the ground.

Take his last patient, for example. He had no idea whether the man had been the aggressor or the victim in the affray that had resulted in his injuries and didn't really care. All he'd been interested in was assessing the severity of the head injury, checking the bloodshot pupils for their reaction to light to gauge the likelihood that he was suffering from concussion and pulling the laceration in his scalp together with a neat row of stitches.

Unfortunately, his patient had been one of those who became combative after a long night of too much alcohol rounded off by some fast food of dubious quality. He'd started swinging punches as soon as Gideon had come towards him with the syringe full of anaesthetic to deaden the wound. Then, coinciding with the very first stitch, came the vomiting episode. Now, as soon as Gideon found some clean clothes, he'd have to try to ascertain whether the nausea had been the result of everything the man had put in his stomach or whether it was a more worrying symptom related to his head injury.

And all the time he would spend sorting out the drunkard's problems, one small part of his brain would be upstairs, wondering why neither of the babies had started putting on weight yet, and worrying whether Adam had finally kicked off the infection that had set him back so dangerously.

'West!' The call was accompanied by a bang on the shower-cubicle door. 'RTA coming in,' a voice informed him, shouting over the drumming of the water. 'Reports say it's a Chelsea tractor stuffed with kids, broadsided when it jumped a set of lights. ETA six minutes.'

'I'll be there,' he called back as he reached out to shut

the water off with one hand and for the towel he'd flicked up over the top of the door with the other.

It wasn't easy dragging a clean set of limp cotton scrubs over wet legs and he could already feel the water trickling down the back of his neck from his wet hair and soaking into the fabric of the V-necked top as he strode back out into a scene of chaos.

The ambulance must have made good time because the first delivery of shocked, tearful children had already arrived in Triage.

'What have we got?' he asked, and the reply was barely audible over the cacophony of sound surrounding him.

'This lot's mainly superficial cuts and bruises, with one Colles' fracture,' he was told by the rather harried member of staff. 'They're mostly shocked by what's happened and, being girls, seem to love making a noisy crisis out of a second-rate drama.'

They were also taking great delight in using their mobile phones to photograph each other and send the results to their friends.

'No telephones!' Gideon barked gruffly, his deeper male voice cutting effortlessly through the shrill girlish squeals as though he'd wielded a well-honed machete through dense undergrowth. 'Switch all your mobiles off *now*, or I'll have to ask you to leave the department.'

A couple of the girls responded immediately, but the other two looked as though they would try to defy him until he focused his best glare on them.

'There is sensitive equipment in a hospital, and the signals from your phones could cause it to malfunction,' he added in a more normal voice, although he knew that the hospital's stated reason for banning mobile phones was largely out of date with the more recent improvements in mobile telephone technology. Still, the lingering rule did mean that the various corridors and waiting areas weren't filled with annoying ring-tones and selfishly loud one-sided conversations.

'If we can't use our phones, how are we supposed to let our parents know to come and get us?' demanded one of the sulkier girls.

'If necessary, we will call them for you,' Sophie, the triage nurse, said. 'But we'll sort all that out once you've been checked over.'

'I've already rung mine,' volunteered another girl with a smug smile. 'She's going to phone all the others in the car pool to let them know where we are and what's happened.'

Gideon stifled a groan. That meant that they had a very limited time in which to get as many of these girls as possible checked over and ready for rapid discharge. It wouldn't be long before they were inundated with hysterical parents responding to a—no doubt very embellished—recounting of that morning's events.

'Right, Sophie,' he said briskly, 'wheel them through into the minor injuries cubicles and let's get them out of here as quickly as possible.'

'What about the other patients who've already been triaged?' she demanded in a hushed voice, no doubt wondering if his decision would cause a riot among the patients already waiting.

Gideon pulled a face, knowing that he didn't want to bring the wrath of the hospital's administrators down on his head if any of the other patients breached the time restraints. 'Direct them to the other members of staff, but if you get any problems, let me know. In that case, the girls—and their parents—will just have to wait. Don't forget, there are still more girls to come, and they'll probably be the more badly injured ones.'

And they hadn't had any information about the other vehicle that had been involved in the crash yet. Were those occupants injured, too, or had they been unlucky enough that they'd be making nothing more than a brief stop in the department before they were taken to the hospital mortuary in the basement of the building.

But there wasn't time to worry about them, not when there were tearful girls with various injuries waiting for his attention.

He'd worked his way through the girls who had injuries that required little more than a temporary dressing and had just finished checking a scalp wound for any stray fragments of windscreen when he glanced up past the edge of the curtain and saw Nadia standing in Triage, covered in blood.

Gideon could have sworn that his own blood froze in his veins at the sight. He knew for certain that his lungs ceased to function at the thought that someone *had* attacked her on her way home.

'Nadia,' he breathed, and only just remembered his responsibilities in time to direct the nurse to use cyano-acrylate glue to close the scalp wound. Then he was out of the cubicle and across the room in a flash.

'Nadia…are you all right? What happened? Were you attacked on your way home?'

'Gideon! No!' Nadia fended him off, doing her best not to smear him with blood when that was the least of his worries.

Why that should be was something he would have to think about later, when his heart wasn't trying to beat its way out through his ribs. For the moment all he knew was that he couldn't bear it if anything had happened to the gentle woman who spent her time taking care of his precious babies.

'I am *not* hurt,' Nadia said firmly, and the words finally penetrated the haze of panic that surrounded him. 'I saw the accident and went to help. This is not my blood. It is the blood of the injured woman in the car.'

'Are you sure?' There was just so much of it that it seemed impossible that some of it wasn't be hers.

'I am sure, Gideon. All I need is somewhere to clean myself before I go home…so I do not scare anyone on the street.'

It was the glimpse of an impish grin that finally persuaded him that she really was uninjured, and it was only then that he realised that his display of concern had made him the focus of practically every one of his colleagues in the department.

'But first,' she added, drawing him away from the surprising realisation that he didn't really care whether the entire hospital was gossiping about him, 'is there some way you can find out what happened to the woman in the car?'

'Which woman?' Gideon had only been seeing the children injured in the crash. He had no idea how many adults had been involved.

'Maria. The passenger in the car that was hit by the van with all the children,' Nadia explained, and Gideon wondered what the woman who owned the expensive vehicle would think if she'd heard it called a van. 'She told me that she and her husband were on their way to the hospital. She was in labour with their first child.'

'I suppose they were hurrying here and didn't see the lights,' he murmured, easily able to visualise the scene and its unintended consequences.

'Not at all,' Nadia corrected him instantly. 'It was the van that ignored the red light. *They* were the ones who caused the accident. I saw it because I was about to cross the road.'

Whatever the rights or wrongs of the situation, no one seemed to have come off completely unscathed, he thought as he made his way to the whiteboard and checked to see if there was a pregnant woman listed.

'There's no one in labour.' He showed Nadia after he untangled the codes required by the hospital's insistence on patient confidentiality. 'Perhaps she was transferred up to the maternity ward.'

He made his way across to Sophie at the triage station, knowing that she had an amazing memory for names and cases.

'Sophie, can you tell me where you sent the pregnant woman who came in from the RTA—Maternity or Theatre?' he asked when she paused to draw breath. 'Her first name was Maria, but I don't have a surname.'

'The RTA with the Chelsea tractor full of kids? Was she a friend of yours?' Sophie asked even as her eyes widened at the blood-spattered state of the woman beside him.

'Not really. Nadia was a bystander at the scene of the accident and wanted to know where to go to visit her.'

'I'm sorry, Nadia, but she didn't make it,' Sophie told her gently. 'The accident caused a tear in the aorta and she bled out before they could get her here. She was dead on arrival.'

'And the baby?' Nadia prompted urgently, even as someone else tried to catch Sophie's attention. 'They were able to save the baby?'

'I'm sorry.' Sophie shook her head and Gideon marvelled that such a busy woman could make the attempt to break such unhappy news as gently as possible. 'I heard that he'd been too long without oxygen by the time they got him out. They couldn't get his heart started.'

'Oh, no!' Gideon saw the colour drain out of Nadia's face. For a moment she swayed on her feet and he wondered briefly if he was going to have to catch her.

He should have known better. A woman who could deal with the high-stress life of dealing with some of the most vulnerable patients in the hospital was bound to be made of sterner stuff. It took her a second or two, but he actually saw her draw on some hidden inner resources to keep herself on her feet.

'Thank you for telling me this,' she said quietly, her formal words sounding almost quaintly old-fashioned in the fast-paced surroundings of a modern A and E department.

'Are you ready to take your next patient?' Sophie asked, almost apologetically. 'We've got several who need to be seen in the next fifteen or twenty minutes.'

Gideon's gaze immediately went to Nadia and his strange need to be there for her warred with his ingrained sense of duty to his profession.

'Go. Do your job, Gideon,' Nadia said, almost as though she was able to read his mind. 'I am all right...or I will be when I can find some soap and water,' she added with a grimace towards her hands. At least her jacket was dark enough that any bloodstains were virtually invisible, but the same couldn't be said for the pale sweater she was wearing underneath it.

'I can get her something to wear,' Sophie suggested quickly, then turned to Nadia with a smile. 'Provided you don't have any objection to wearing mismatched tops and bottoms from some sets of prototype uniforms that got left in the cupboard a while ago?'

Gideon left them discussing the vagaries of hospital administrators trying to design nurses' uniforms when they had little idea of the needs of the people who would be wearing them, but it was the lost expression in Nadia's eyes that followed him into the few quiet moments during that shift.

He could appreciate that her soft heart would grieve at the thought of a precious little life being lost through a driver's moment of stupidity, but the more he thought about it, the more he came to believe that there had been something deeper behind the look she'd worn...something that had resonated personally with her.

Was there something in her past? he wondered as he waited for a translator to explain the need for his elderly Bangladeshi patient to be admitted to hospital urgently for treatment to a foot that was rapidly heading towards gangrene, the result of undiagnosed diabetes.

Perhaps something that had happened to Nadia in her own country...something serious enough that it had left her with that air of sadness under her gentle cheerfulness?

And what were the chances that she would ever speak about it, when she didn't even trust him enough to allow him to give her a lift in the pouring rain? Slim to non-existent, he admitted wryly, but that wouldn't stop him from offering, especially after that shock today. He'd honestly believed that she'd been attacked when he'd seen her standing there, covered in blood.

His thoughts ground to a sudden halt as he suddenly realised that something fundamental had changed. For the last few weeks, ever since his two babies had been born, almost every thought that had come into his head had begun and ended with their welfare. If most of his thoughts about Nadia had been in relation to the fact that she was taking care of Adam and Amy with the sort of dedication that she would show if they were her own children.

At least, that had been the case until he'd seen her standing there and had been convinced that something awful had happened to her. And, just like that, the concern he'd been feeling towards her—concern that he'd convinced himself was just a normal caring human trait—had crystallised into something deeper, something far more personal. And thinking about his reaction now, he was startled to realise just how much the idea had affected him, how empty his days would feel if, for some reason, she was no longer a part of them.

'Mr Dhasmana will be going up to the ward as soon as there is a bed free,' the translator reported, snapping Gideon's attention back to his patient in a hurry. 'His wife will be taken home by their daughter to collect his personal belongings, but she is having difficulty accepting that she will not be staying here with him to take care of him.' The young translator leaned towards Gideon to add in a lower voice, 'This is what would have happened back in the region where they came from, many years ago, where quite often family members would perform nursing duties for patients.'

'Perhaps you could suggest that she should use the next few days to rest, ready for when her husband comes home again,' Gideon offered with a smile for the anxious woman. 'Several nights without him snoring in the house will be good for her.'

He knew the exact moment when that final sentence was translated because both husband and wife laughed and the tense atmosphere in the room grew lighter.

The fact that the elderly woman had been prepared to camp out on the floor beside her husband's bed returned to him at intervals during the remaining hours of his shift, and made him realise that he'd been doing something similar in his vigil beside Adam and Amy. In his case, his presence hadn't been because he thought he would be needed to take care of their feeding or their personal hygiene, but because he'd been convinced that something dreadful would happen if he wasn't there every second to *will* them to survive.

Well, with him or without him, the two of them were still alive, and even though neither of them had made any great progress so far, at least they hadn't had any bleeding into their brains, their lungs slowly seemed to be increasing in capacity so that it wasn't quite so hard to keep up the oxygen levels in their blood, and their hearts were beating strongly. And if a large part of that was due to Nadia's dedication to their care, it was only another reason why he found his thoughts returning to her again and again.

* * *

Nadia heard the security lock on the unit's outer door being activated and her pulse rate began to go up even before she recognised Gideon's footsteps coming along the corridor towards her.

'You are a crazy woman,' she muttered under her breath, deliberately keeping her back towards the door so that she wouldn't be able to watch him scrub his hands and don gloves and apron. 'Apart from the fact that he's a man, and you have sworn to have nothing more to do with them, he is the father of your patients and only comes here to be with *them*, not to be with you.'

Except…it had seemed like genuine concern for her welfare when he'd hurried towards her in A and E, thinking that she'd been injured. Perhaps that was just because he was worried who would care for Amy and Adam if she was unable to, but she didn't believe that for a moment. The Gideon West she was starting to know wasn't that shallow.

He also wasn't one of those doctors who just went through the motions to earn his salary. From the conversations they'd had, over the last week or so, she'd heard enough to know that, for him, medicine was far more than just a job. In fact, the more she learned about him, the more she discovered there was to admire…and she hadn't thought she would ever be able to say that about a man.

'How are they?' he asked from right behind her, but she wasn't in the least bit startled because she'd known that he was there without hearing a single step because it seemed as if every pore in her skin was sensitive to his presence. Then she detected the warm waft of shampoo and soap that told her he'd had a shower before he'd come to the unit, and for the first time in her life she found herself imagining what he would look like with nothing more than droplets of water and rivulets of foam running over his body.

She shook her head to banish the images and it was only when she saw the flash of panic in Gideon's eyes that she realised how he'd interpreted her action.

'No. I am sorry,' she said hurriedly. 'They are well.' And only then noticed that she'd actually reached out to put a reassuring hand over his clenched fist.

Nadia stared at the point of contact in disbelief.

What was the matter with her? She was in the middle of cleaning around the sites where various needles entered their tiny bodies, a job that required strict hygiene to minimise the risk of introducing infection, and she'd just forgotten herself so much that she'd contaminated her gloves.

'Excuse me!' she gasped as she snatched her hand back and immediately started to strip the glove off, her fumbling attempt making it obvious that she was now trembling from head to foot. 'I must…I need to…' To her mortification she wasn't even able to put a single sentence together, overwhelmingly aware that those intense green eyes were watching her every clumsy move.

'Nadia, it's all right,' he soothed, but that only made things worse because she could tell just how concerned he was that he might have upset her in some way. She needed to reassure him that wasn't the case but what could she say? She couldn't tell him how frightening it was to find herself reacting to nothing more then his presence in a room, and she certainly couldn't tell him why the fact that she'd just voluntarily touched him had made her shake.

'You…you startled me,' she managed, grabbing for the first excuse she could think of. She took a step back from him and then another, but the cot behind her prevented her from putting any more space between them even though she felt she needed it if she was ever going to be able to breathe evenly again. She certainly couldn't draw in a lungful that was so full of the essence of Gideon without her body reacting in such crazy ways, and if he should notice… 'I was concentrating and…'

Those gorgeous green eyes were too intelligent and far too intent for her peace of mind, especially when his steady gaze was accompanied by a frown that drew those straight dark brows together. Realising that her flustered reaction had attracted his attention, she stifled a swearword that she hadn't even thought about in years, let alone used.

The last thing she needed was for him to see her as anything other than the person who was caring for his babies' needs. If he started asking questions and she had to be evasive…well, she didn't think it would take more than a moment or two for him to see though any ambiguous answers she might give, and there was no way that she could tell him the truth about herself, not if she wanted to keep her job. She certainly wouldn't trust her babies to the sort of woman she'd once been.

'It's nearly time for my break,' she said, inspired by a glance at the clock on the wall behind him. At least that would give her a chance to get away from him and try to get her head on straight. After all, he wasn't likely to want to leave Amy and Adam so soon after getting here.

Except she was wrong.

Much to her surprise, when she finished all her immediate tasks and handed over the babies' care to Monica, she found Gideon close on her heels when she left the nursery to make her way to their little staff-room, and the determined expression on his face told her that he intended getting some answers.

Well, he wasn't going to be successful because there were some things that she would never be able to tell him…never be able to speak of to anyone who hadn't been there.

So, she would just have to sidetrack him with the one topic that they *could* share—Amy and Adam. Perhaps she could ask him a question about his preparations for the day when he would be taking them home?

'Tell me what's wrong,' he demanded as soon as the door closed behind the two of them.

'Wrong?' she parroted, completely caught on the hop by the fact that he'd taken the lead in a conversation that she'd never intended starting. Unfortunately, his agenda wasn't the same as hers.

'Either there's something wrong with the babies, or with you,' he insisted. 'And as you've just told me that neither Adam nor Amy is doing anything to cause concern, that means the problem's with you…unless *I've* done something to upset you,' he added as a sudden afterthought, his frown returning full force. 'Is that what it is?'

CHAPTER FIVE

'No, GIDEON. It's nothing you've done,' she denied swiftly, struck by guilt that he should have thought for a moment that any of this was *his* fault.

In spite of the fact that they'd clashed wills on several occasions, mostly over her concern for the state of his health, he had shown her nothing other than professional respect and consideration. He'd even voiced his admiration for her skills in dealing with such tiny babies and reinforced her pride in her chosen profession, so she couldn't allow him to think that he might have done anything to upset her. It just wouldn't be right.

But that left her with the impossible task of explaining her reaction to him, of finding an acceptable reason why she was doing her best to maintain as much distance between them as she could, especially when she was rapidly beginning to feel as if she just wanted to be closer to him.

She had never envisaged a time when she might want to be close to a man, but that had been before she'd met Gideon West and witnessed his devotion to those two precious beings in the room along the corridor.

Then there was the way he'd offered her a lift home

for no reason other then the fact it had been raining heavily and she would be walking through one of the less salubrious parts of the city. She could almost make herself discount the fact that he'd hurried to her side when he'd seen her appear blood-spattered in A and E. That could have been nothing more than his automatic reaction due to his medical training.

However, none of that explained her own reaction to the man when she'd touched him.

She'd felt a strange shivery heat shimmer through her, making her aware of everywhere that her clothes touched her body even as it had begun to coil deep inside her. And for the first time ever there'd been a sensation of…of excitement…of anticipation, almost.

Oh, it was so hard to describe it when she'd never felt anything like it before, and the most confusing thing of all was that she didn't know whether she should be welcoming it or not. On past experience, there was nothing about being close to a man that had ever ended well for her…

'Nadia?'

She felt the swift wash of colour come into her cheeks when she realised that she must have been staring at him while her thoughts scurried along their own tangled paths.

Not that he wasn't worth staring at. He certainly was, with those penetrating green eyes surrounded by the sort of long dark lashes that were wasted on a man, all set in a face that had the rugged sort of symmetry that any camera would love. His dark hair was longer these days than it had been the first day he'd rushed to his babies' sides, as though his life was too full now for frequent visits to a barber.

'I'm sorry,' she gasped, suddenly realising that she was in danger of—what was it the younger nurses called it, zoning out? 'I was just…I didn't mean to—'

She nearly groaned aloud in relief when she heard the sharp intrusive tones of the paging device clipped to the narrow leather belt circling his lean waist.

'Damn thing,' he muttered as he reached for the nearby phone. 'Don't they realise I'm not on duty?'

Given the time Gideon had arrived in the unit, Nadia knew that he'd already worked several hours beyond his shift today. That was, if he'd come straight up here the way he usually did, she added to herself, wondering at the sudden sharp stab of…*something* at the thought that he might not have come straight up, that he might have gone somewhere else and spoken to someone else, perhaps someone beautiful and willing to smile and listen attentively while he poured out all his worries about his tiny babies and their fight for life.

As if she had any right to have any feelings one way or the other about what Gideon West did when he was out of the unit. She was just the nurse who was taking care of his babies after all, she reminded herself fiercely, even as she fought to drag her eyes away from his frowning face.

'Stupid idiot!' he snarled as he returned the handset to its cradle with a sharp click.

'Is there a problem?' she found herself asking, unable to prevent herself caring that he was obviously angry about something.

'Petty bureaucracy,' he growled as he dragged one hand through his hair, leaving it sticking up in all directions like a little boy's. Adam's hair might do the same thing in a few years, perhaps, and she felt a swift pang that she would never be there to see it.

'What happened?' She had to drag her thoughts back to what he'd said. She had no right to feel regrets that she'd never see those precious babies growing up. All she had was a duty to do her part to try to get them strong enough to leave the unit.

'Two of my patients were in A and E longer than the permitted time, so some pencil-neck paged me to rap me over the knuckles!' he exclaimed in evident disgust. 'He was totally uninterested in the fact that it was in their best interests not to be moved in the middle of potentially lifesaving procedures.'

'Perhaps he is only doing his job?' she suggested, even as she revelled in the fire of his commitment towards his patients. This was one way in which the two of them were equals.

'He would do better if he spent his time chasing the subcontractors they employed to do the cleaning,' he said darkly. 'Better still, he should get down on his hands and knees and clean the muck that accumulates in the corners when they do nothing more than flop a glorified dry duster around a room. Then he could make a start on disinfecting and scrubbing all the hidden nooks and crannies in the trauma rooms. You wouldn't believe the infectious muck that can build up... Ah, hell, I'm sorry. I shouldn't rant at you like that. It's hardly your fault that the politicians made a complete mess of everything when they started sticking their noses into things they don't understand.'

'So, you think the politicians should just keep providing more and more public money? You don't think they have a duty to the people who elected them to oversee whether it's being spent properly?' She fought a grin as she posed the questions most calculated to heat up the discussion, suddenly realising that it was possible to enjoy the fact that she was arguing with a man.

'Of course they should have some system in place to make sure that the money isn't wasted,' he conceded swiftly, 'but that certainly doesn't mean that they should censure a doctor for doing his best for his patient.' His eyes flashed fervently green from under those straight dark brows. 'They do not—and *can*not—have the right to go against a doctor's clinical decision…and certainly not just because it doesn't fit in with their tick-box mentality.'

Suddenly, he seemed to realise just how heated he'd become and he pulled a rueful face.

'Sorry about the rant,' he apologised, and she felt quite guilty that she was grateful that the topic had apparently made him forget his previous question.

'I don't know very much about the hospital politics, especially in the way it affects a department such as A and E,' she admitted. 'I know there is sometimes a problem with the standards of the cleaners supplied by the contractors, but I was told that some companies try to cut corners and make the cleaners hurry through their work far too fast to do a good job. Not that it would happen in this department,' she added quickly. 'Mr Weatherby would never allow that.' She gave a brief laugh at the thought. 'I think he would prefer to throw them out and do the job himself rather than risk the lives of our little patients.'

'And you'd probably be there right beside him with a scrubbing brush,' Gideon said, and for a moment she was surprised how accurately he'd guessed, almost frightened that he seemed to be getting to know her so well that he could predict how she would respond in such a situation. She was frightened, too, that the expression of approval she saw in his eyes should mean so much to her.

It wasn't supposed to matter to her. It had been years since she'd decided that the last thing she needed or wanted was the approval of some man…*any* man. And it had been so easy to stick to that decision ever since she'd managed to get away from Laszlo.

So, how was it that Gideon seemed to have managed to slip inside her defences? How was it that a warm expression in those gorgeous green eyes could make her quiver like a puppy when its master praised it for performing a clever trick? Had she learned nothing that she could stand here and feel gratitude that he approved of what he saw in her?

'I must get back to the nursery,' she said, and only realised just how abrupt she must have sounded when he blinked and frowned at her. Well, she thought as she exited the room rapidly, feeling his eyes burning into her back as she went, it was too late to change the tone of her voice now, but if she was lucky it wasn't too late for her to shore up her defences again.

It was lonely behind the wall that separated her from danger…so very lonely…but if she stayed where it was safe, kept her silvery blonde hair dyed this unflattering shade of brown and wore the contact lenses that darkened her blue eyes to a hazel brown, then Laszlo wouldn't be able to find her again and take her back to the life she'd hated so much.

* * *

'I wonder what *that* was about?' Gideon muttered under his breath as he watched Nadia walk swiftly away from him. For a moment it seemed almost as if she would break into a run in her effort to leave the room as fast as possible, but she had that nurse's swift gait down perfectly.

Everything inside him wanted to follow her…to demand some answers…but there had been something in her eyes…something as wary as a wounded animal that warned him that he would do better to back off for a moment and think out his strategy.

'Strategy? What strategy?' he scoffed, suddenly re-alising how ludicrous his thoughts had become. Nadia was the specialist nurse caring for his vulnerable babies, not someone he should be seeing as a woman he was interested in and wanted to pursue and who therefore needed placating if he had upset her in some way.

Except…

Except, without him realising how it had happened, he suddenly realised just how much he *was* interested in her.

That took the wind out of him and he felt strangely breathless as he lowered himself into the nearest chair.

Surely he was mistaken.

His feelings must be mixed up in the gratitude he felt for the dedication she showed towards caring for his babies, not for her personally.

Except…

Except all he had to do was picture her quiet smile and his heart gave a stupid extra beat, and when he re-membered the awful dark emptiness he'd seen in those strangely hypnotic hazel eyes, all he'd wanted to do was banish whatever memories had put it there and keep her safe.

As if she'd let him, he realised with a wry smile. Nadia had to be one of the most independent women he'd ever met, as well as one of the most secretive.

He cast his mind back over the few weeks he'd known her and had to admit that she'd told him absolutely nothing about herself. He knew nothing more about her than he had when he'd been introduced to her on the day of Adam and Amy's birth—that her name was Nadia Smith and she was a specialist nurse. He didn't even know what country she'd been born in or the name of the language that had given her speech that exotic lilt.

But he would like to know, he realised with bone-deep certainty. For some unexplained reason he found himself fascinated by her and was struck by an urgent need to know everything there was to know about her.

Where had she been born? Did she have family there? What had prompted her to choose to leave her homeland to come to London? Did she intend staying here or...or was there someone waiting for her to return?

That last thought made him feel as though a fist had suddenly tightened around his heart.

Was *that* why she didn't tell him anything about herself...because there was a man who loved her waiting for her return? Was her love for this unknown man the reason why she seemed to deliberately maintain a careful distance between the two of *them*?

Everything inside him wanted to deny the very idea, but then he just had to remember the sudden edginess between the two of them a few minutes ago to realise that it was all too possible.

Had she felt that he'd encroached on the invisible boundary she'd erected around herself? Was that why she'd hurried away—because she didn't want to have to spell things out for him?

For several minutes he sat there staring blankly into space while he tried to come to terms with the strange empty feeling that had just opened up inside him. It was a shock to discover that the idea that he had lost Nadia before she was ever his could hurt him more than the ending of his marriage.

'That's crazy!' he whispered.

And it *was* crazy, if he thought about it logically. He and Norah had known each other for nearly a year before they'd married, and once they'd realised that they were never going to be able to have the family they'd wanted as easily as they'd expected, things had grown tense very rapidly. With the clear vision of hindsight, he could see that the fact that it had been her body that was failing her that had caused the almost frenetic desperation to take hold of her, but at the time he'd come to resent the way she'd begun to treat him as little more than a means of providing the sperm she'd needed for her next attempt at achieving the all-important pregnancy. Even before they'd embarked along the route towards surrogacy he should have realised that their marriage had been in serious trouble...or perhaps it was because he *had* realised that it would take something that desperate that he'd agreed to the idea. In the event, Norah's demand for a divorce had coincided exactly with the confirmation of a pregnancy in which she'd no longer wanted any part.

So, after such a harrowing end to something that had

started with love and hope, how could he possibly think that he might be ready to find another woman desirable enough to want to begin the whole process again?

He felt his eyes widen as the words formed inside his brain.

Was that really the way his mind was working? After such a short time, was he really so attracted to the quiet, self-contained Nadia that he was actually considering pursuing her as a potential…what? A potential bed partner? A wife? A mother for his children?

Whoa, he thought in sudden panic. This was getting uncomfortably heavy, especially when she'd just cut him off at the knees.

He drew in a deep steadying breath to try to force his racing pulse to slow down, but it was a waste of time because every time he thought about the possibility of having Nadia in his life it started to gallop again.

Be calm and logical about it, he counselled himself.

For a start, he didn't know anything about the person Nadia was outside the unit, so how could he possibly know whether she was someone he wanted as part of his and his children's lives? Of course, he knew just how dedicated she was to her job, and that her protective instincts were strong enough that she'd been willing to stop and help when she'd witnessed that RTA the other day.

But since he'd seen the shadows in her eyes, he also knew that she had a past that he knew nothing about, secrets that could mean that any relationship between the two of them was impossible, no matter how much he might want it.

So, what was he going to do about it?

He stifled the urge to laugh at that thought, knowing that it was totally against his nature *not* to try to do something to achieve his aims.

First, he was going to have to get Nadia to open up to him, and to do that he had a feeling that he was going to have to find some way to get her to trust him enough to tell him her secrets.

'Well, you could hardly expect to have a long-term relationship with someone you didn't know well,' he muttered reasonably, then grimaced at the irony of that thought. He'd believed that he'd known Norah well, once upon a time. Otherwise he wouldn't have proposed to her. But how could he have known that being thwarted in her desire to carry a child would have come to dominate her every waking thought so that nothing—not him, their love or their marriage—had mattered to her any more when she hadn't been able to achieve it.

Did Nadia's reticence hide such a secret? Or perhaps there was something about *him* that attracted women with hidden agendas.

'You don't even know whether she's hiding any-thing,' he reminded himself with a swift return to logic. The shadows he'd seen might be nothing more than the memories of a love affair gone wrong. That could even be the reason why she'd left her own country and come to London to nurse.

'But you won't know unless you find some way to get her to open up to you,' he said under his breath as his solitude was broken by two members of the unit coming in search of a reviving cup of coffee.

And for *that* he was going to need patience, he realised as he made his way into the nursery, freshly scrubbed, gowned and gloved, and received not so much as the briefest glance in his direction.

'Let me help,' he offered when he saw that once more Nadia was concentrating on disentangling some of Adam's vital lines from Amy's grasping hands. He leaned forward over the crib to get a better view and almost stepped back again when he felt the way she stiffened when he accidentally brushed against her.

At the last moment he realised that accustoming her to his proximity might be one way to persuade her that she didn't have to be afraid to open up to him. Well, it was the best idea he'd come up with yet, he rationalised, deliberately shoving to the back of his mind the fact that he didn't really need an excuse to want to be close to the soft fresh scent that surrounded her, or to relish the intermittent contact between her slender arm and his darker, hair-roughened one.

'Can I hold one of them while you sort the other one out?' he offered, and for a moment his preoccupation with their nurse was banished by the hope that he might be able to cradle one of his precious babies again.

'Do you think you might be able to manage both of them?' Nadia asked with what sounded suspiciously like a challenge in her voice.

'Both at once?' It was hard to force the words past the lump in his throat. He had held both of them, separately, several times, but it would be the first time that he'd had both of them in his arms simultaneously. Did this mean that they were finally making serious progress?

'Sit down and make yourself comfortable,' she

ordered briskly, but he'd caught a hint of a smile before she'd controlled it.

Then the only thing he was noticing was how impossibly small and fragile his two babies still were, in spite of all the care and attention that had been lavished on them since their birth.

Even with both of them in his arms, they weighed practically nothing and still looked just like two baby birds that had fallen out of a nest.

'Hello, Adam. Hello, Amy,' he said, his voice barely above a whisper it was so full of emotion. 'Your daddy finally got his hands on both of you at once.'

He marvelled anew at the perfection of their little starfish hands and noticed that their eyelashes seemed to have grown longer and darker since the last time he'd held either of them.

Selfishly, he was glad that they both seemed to have inherited their hair colour from him, rather than the birth mother who Norah had chosen partly because the woman's hair and eyes had matched her own. It was too soon to be sure whether their eyes would stay the blue they had been at birth or would change to his own more unusual green. Not that it really mattered, because he loved them both just the way they were, grateful that they had come into his life, no matter how traumatic their arrival had been.

The sudden flash of the camera wielded by Nadia was the only thing that stopped the sudden threat of tears of gratitude from falling.

'I thought you ought to have a photo to mark this special occasion,' she said as she checked the image she'd captured. 'Perfect,' she pronounced in a slightly more husky tone and he realised that there was something different in her expression...a softness that hadn't been there just a short while ago.

'May I see?' he asked, wondering if it was something about the picture she'd taken with the camera kept specifically for such landmark moments that had wrought the change.

He was almost disappointed when she angled the camera towards him and he saw nothing remarkable in the digital display. In fact, it looked like nothing more than the expected image of a new father holding two tiny premature babies, until he realised that she'd managed to capture the very moment when his heart had been in danger of overflowing with love for these precious children.

He had to clear his throat before he could speak, and even then he couldn't meet her eyes, knowing that she'd recognised the fact that he'd nearly betrayed his emotions in such a public manner.

'Could you print an extra copy?' he asked, knowing that he still sounded choked by emotion in spite of his best efforts. 'I'd like to take one home to put in the album I'm making...so they can see themselves when they're older.'

'Of course I can,' she said immediately, and he dared to glance up just in time to catch a glimpse of tears sparkling in her eyes, too.

Why was Gideon making it so hard for her? Nadia grumbled silently as she trudged towards the entrance of A and E.

Ever since the day she'd seen him sitting there with those two precious babies in his arms for the first time, the expression of utter devotion on his face had never left her mind for a moment.

She'd never dreamed that there could be a man who could feel things so deeply that he was moved close to tears. In fact, she'd never met a man who was in any way like Gideon West, and that made it harder than she would have believed to resist him.

So, here she was, arriving nearly an hour early for her shift, having set her alarm to get up in time to make a batch of something he'd called flapjacks so that he could have a taste of a favourite treat from his childhood.

Was this the way to maintain a safe distance between the two of them? Definitely not. But when the man was even invading her dreams with his smiling eyes, making her think of sunlight flickering through fresh green leaves, and when the rebellious curls at the back of his longer-than-ever hair were tempting her to run her fingers through them to feel if they were as silky soft as they looked, how *could* she resist him?

Now all she had to do was find some way of giving him the treat she'd baked without his colleagues noticing. The last thing she wanted to do was cause him embarrassment in front of the people with whom he worked.

She'd already heard rumours on the hospital grapevine that some of the more predatory nurses in the hospital were willing to put up with the existence of the two babies hanging on to life in the premature baby unit if it meant that had a chance of getting their claws into one of the most attractive single men on the staff. She certainly didn't need to have her own name added to the list, not if she was going to keep herself out of the public gaze.

She was so busy wondering if she was going to be able to see Gideon without others noticing she was there that Nadia completely forgot to look where she was going and almost cannoned into a man who was coming out of the department.

It was the vicious way he was berating his young female companion that first sent the rush of horror raising her hackles. The brief terrified glance she dared to throw in his direction was enough to bring her out in a cold sweat as she swiftly turned her face away from him and hunched the shoulder closest to him to hide as much of her jaw as she could.

It was Laszlo! Here in her hospital! The words were shrieking inside her head so loudly that she was amazed everyone couldn't hear them, too.

CHAPTER SIX

How had Laszlo found her? What was he doing in England? Had he used his drugs connections to track her down or had it just been sheer bad luck that had sent him here at the precise moment she was entering A and E?

Most importantly, had she been quick enough to turn her head or had he seen her…recognised her in spite of her efforts to disguise herself?

Her heart was beating so hard and so fast that she thought she was going to be sick. How she'd managed to hold on to the little plastic box containing the treat she'd made for Gideon, she had no idea. Her hands were shaking so much that she was barely able to make them grip the smooth surfaces.

'Nadia! What a nice surprise!' Gideon said right beside her and she was so grateful for the obvious pleasure in his voice that she nearly collapsed into his arms.

'G-Gideon…' Even she could hear the way her teeth were chattering too much to say his name properly.

'Hey…what's the matter?' he asked, even as he wrapped a warmly supportive arm around her shoulders and began to guide her along the corridor. 'You didn't witness another accident, did you?'

'N-no.' She shook her head jerkily, torn between hiding her face in the broad shoulder just inches away from her and looking back to make sure that Laszlo wasn't standing on the other side of A and E Reception, trying to get a better look at her.

'Are you sick, then? In pain?'

The memories of the misery that man had put her through were enough to make her feel sick for the rest of her life, but she knew that wasn't what Gideon meant.

'Nadia, say something, please. You're frightening me,' he said, and his concern for her was so clear that she was finally able to make herself speak.

'I—I'm not ill,' she reassured him, even as she tried to find the right words to explain away the fact that she must look as if she'd nearly come face to face with her worst nightmare. 'I just…I just had a bit of a shock… nearly bumped into some I once knew…someone I'd rather not see.'

Those green eyes were far too intelligent as they flicked over her face and when she saw that smiling mouth tighten into a grim line she knew that he had understood far more than she'd wanted him to know.

'It was the man who hurt you,' he said flatly, and she knew there was no point in denying it. After all, he was right, up to a point.

'Yes,' she whispered miserably, already mourning the consequences of that brief accidental encounter. If Laszlo had seen her…recognised her…then there was no way that she could stay here…no way she could take the risk that he might grab her one day when she was on her way to work and—

'Do you want me to call the police?' Gideon's voice

broke into her tangled thoughts and sent them scattering to the four winds. 'You know that if he's stalking you, you could take out a restraining order or something.'

'No! No police!' she exclaimed urgently. They wouldn't be able to help, no one would be able to help if Laszlo found her.

'Are you sure, sweetheart?' His hands on her shoulders were warm and comforting and finally managed to dispel the worst of the trembling...until the endearment he'd used suddenly registered.

Oh, it was just so unfair, she lamented silently, even as that one precious word lit a tiny spark in the dark corner of her soul. The very first time that someone had called her something so beautiful, and it had to be on the day that all the ugliest parts of her life had come back to haunt her.

She'd actually begun to wonder if she dared to let herself hope for a normal life...to imagine that Gideon would be the one man to whom she could spill all the terrible memories and he wouldn't turn away from her in horror.

Now she would never know because, much as she wanted to stay where she could see Gideon every day...at least until Amy and Adam were strong enough to leave the unit...she didn't dare to risk it. There was no way that she could ever go back to the life she had known with Laszlo.

'Do you want to wait here until I finish my shift?' Gideon asked. 'With any luck, I shouldn't be more than half an hour. Then I could see you home.'

Mention of the time drew her eyes to the clock on the wall and her eyes widened in horror.

'I'm going to be late!' she exclaimed. 'I need to get up to the unit or there'll be no one to take care of Amy and Adam.'

'Are you sure you're up to it?' he demanded with a frown, examining her face intently. 'Wouldn't you rather call in sick and go home until you get over your shock?'

Would she rather risk walking home when there was a chance that Laszlo might be loitering somewhere outside, just waiting to follow her, or would she prefer to go up to the security and safety of the unit where only staff and parents who knew the security code could gain entrance? There was no question where she'd rather be.

'I'll be better if I can keep busy,' she said as she struggled out of the squashy chair one-handed, only then realising that she was still holding that small plastic box. 'I brought this for you,' she added awkwardly, silently wishing that she'd never succumbed to the temptation to make the treat for him. If she hadn't made the flapjacks, she'd never have been coming through the door to A and E and would never have come anywhere near Laszlo.

'For me?' He took the box gingerly, clearly intrigued.

She found herself holding her breath as he peeled the lid back and peered inside.

'Flapjacks!' he exclaimed with a smile of delight that sent a burst of pure joy through her that almost made the unexpected consequences of the gift worthwhile.

He hung his nose over the box and breathed in deeply, drawing in the scents of oats and butter and honey with an expression of boyish bliss before breaking off a bit of one and popping it into his mouth.

Once more her imagination projected Gideon's expression of uninhibited pleasure onto the face of the child that Adam would become, and with each new picture that formed in her head, the ache of knowing that she would never be there to see the event in person deepened.

'Perfect…' he breathed, then, with a look of regret, sealed the lid back down over the golden-brown squares and held it out to her. 'If you insist on going up to work, will you take this up to the unit with you?' He angled a thumb over his shoulder towards his colleagues in A and E. 'That lot will scoff the lot if I leave them down here, but if you promise to look after them, I promise to share them with you when I finish my shift.'

Nadia knew there was no point in spending any more time with him than she had to, but the knowledge that she would be leaving soon, and that once she was gone she would never see him again, made her greedy for every last moment in his company.

'How do you know you can trust me not to "scoff" them without you?' she challenged, then blinked at the fact that it actually sounded as if she was flirting with him. She hadn't even realised that she knew how to do that because she'd never done it before.

And it had felt good, she realised as she flew up the stairs towards the unit, the excited little bubbles in her bloodstream seeming to lend wings to her feet. And the part that had felt particularly special had been the gleam in Gideon's eyes when he'd threatened dire consequences if she ate his flapjacks, and she hadn't even thought about cowering away from him in fear that he would really attack her.

That had been a real revelation. The fact that already she felt as if she knew the man he was enough to know that he wasn't the sort to raise his hand against a woman. The fact that already she knew that she could trust him to treat her with respect and gentleness.

And then her heart bled with the knowledge that it was a waste of time dreaming foolish dreams that this trust might one day be able to undo the deeper damage that had been done to her at Laszlo's hands. She knew that any such dreams would die when she left Gideon because there would never be anyone she could learn to trust the way she was beginning to count on him.

Anyway, for the short time she had left, she needed to focus all her concentration on Amy and Adam; do her best to make sure they were as safe and healthy as possible for the person who would replace her as their carer. And if that thought felt as if it was pulling her heart out by the roots, well, she would just have to live with it because she really didn't have any other options.

'Hey, beautiful babies, how are you doing today?' she crooned as she reached in to stroke a gentle finger over each tiny fist, marvelling at the perfection of each minute fingernail when both babies stretched their hands wide in response to her touch.

'I hope you had a restful night,' she continued as she carefully checked the connections on each monitor and the patency of each line going in and coming out of their little bodies. It wouldn't do to let any of them become blocked—that could do serious damage to their systems.

One of the monitors issued a staccato warning and she wagged a finger at Amy. 'You're not interfering with your brother's wires again, are you?' she said as she checked them again, frowning when everything seemed to be fine.

Another glance at the screen full of displays told her that this time it was one of Amy's sensors that had triggered the alarm.

'Hey, pretty girl, what's the matter with you, then?' she asked as she put gentle fingers on the baby's forehead, testing the truth of the figures that insisted that her temperature was rising. 'You're a little bit warm, aren't you, darling?' she murmured as she made preparations to take a set of samples. 'We need to get these off to the labs as soon as possible to find out what's going on.'

'What *is* going on?' Gideon demanded, and nearly sent her into orbit. She'd been so totally concentrated on what she was doing for Amy that she hadn't even heard the door of the unit opening, let alone tracked the sound of his feet as he'd walked towards her.

'The monitors say that Amy's running a temperature,' she told him, hoping she sounded calmer than she felt. Not only was she worried about what was wrong with his little daughter but the freshly showered man standing so close to her was seriously compromising her own pulse rate and blood pressure.

His face was newly shaven and his damp hair still bore the traces of where he'd impatiently run his fingers through it, and it took a real effort for her to keep her mind on what she was saying when all she could think about was reaching up to tidy the thick strands falling over his forehead.

'I've just taken a set of samples to send up to the lab,' she said when she managed to drag her eyes back to the row of vials.

'I'll take them for you—I'm already taking a set up for Rani,' offered Julia, the young woman who'd only joined the unit that week, and when Nadia saw the hungry expression in her new colleague's eyes as she ran them over Gideon's body she was startled by the feeling of possessiveness that made her want to push the younger woman away.

Mine, she wanted to declare, even though she knew she had no right to, and suddenly realised that for the first time in her life she was experiencing jealousy over knowing that Julia would still be there to smile up at him when *she* was gone.

It seemed to take for ever for the results to come back and the news was bad.

'NEC?' Gideon repeated, his face grey with shock when Josh gave him the news.

Nadia felt sick at such a diagnosis.

Necrotising enterocolitis was one of the more serious conditions that such premature babies were prone to, with whole sections of their intestines succumbing to raging inflammation before the tissues became necrotic and died. The treatment for even moderate attacks could involve extensive invasive surgery, affected lengths of intestines being cut away to prevent it spreading any further.

Some babies didn't survive, and the thought that this might be Amy's fate, perfect little Amy who already had so much character and determination...

Nadia gazed down at the little girl while Josh and Gideon spoke about scans and MRI to determine the extent of the problem, and was struck that something just didn't seem right about the situation. Unfortunately, in the course of her career she'd nursed other babies with NEC and had grown accustomed to watching the rapid progression from the first, almost innocuous rise in temperature to the point where intervention or death became inevitable.

In Amy's case, something just didn't ring true.

On the other side of the room, for example, Rani's temperature was far higher and she looked far more like a candidate for NEC than Amy did, but as far as she knew, Rani's tests had all come back negative.

She gasped as a sudden thought struck her, but when Gideon and Josh both turned to her with questioning looks, she almost didn't dare voice her idea. After all, she was only the nurse, albeit a specialist in the care of premature babies, while both of them were doctors and Josh, in particular, was the unit's consultant.

'What is it?' Gideon said urgently, obviously ready to grasp at anything if it would help Amy.

'Would it be possible to run another set of tests—as a precaution?' she suggested tentatively. 'They could go to the lab while you're doing the scan and MRI and the results should all come in together if you get them put to the front of the queue.'

'What are you thinking?' Gideon asked, and her heart swelled when she realised that he hadn't questioned her right to make suggestions for a second.

'Take the samples.' Josh, too, seemed willing to trust her instincts, after a long silent look at the little girl lying so helpless in the cot with her brother. 'I'll do the paperwork and follow it up with a phone call to hurry things along.'

Nadia hated having to let Amy leave the department without her, but she couldn't leave Adam to anyone else's care just to stand there helplessly while his sister was scrutinised by one high-tech machine after another.

Anyway, she had her hands full trying to calm the little boy who began to cry almost as soon as the department door closed behind his sister.

'Hey, Nadia,' called Julia from across the room. 'Could you come here for a minute and show me what I've done wrong with these monitors? They just seem to keep going off for no reason.'

'I'll be back in a minute, precious,' Nadia murmured to Adam, but he was wailing so angrily that she doubted that he heard her.

'Sorry to be a nuisance but I was so busy looking at Dr Gorgeous that I might have crossed some wires or something,' Julia said as she stepped back to allow Nadia access to the cot and the bank of displays. 'I know Rani isn't very well,' she chattered on as Nadia ran a careful eye over every sensor and lead. 'I seem to be running backwards and forwards to the lab every five minutes with samples for testing... But now the temperature monitor keeps going off and—'

'Page Mr Weatherby,' Nadia interrupted urgently as she sped across the room to grab a trolley specially kitted out with all the equipment needed to keep monitors functioning during a trip from one department to another.

'What?' Julia said gormlessly. 'Why?'

'You need to tell him that he's got the wrong baby,' Nadia said as she swiftly disconnected everything connecting Rani to the department monitors and oxygen supply and reconnected them to the portable system.

Julia was still standing there with her mouth open when Nadia glanced in her direction, and she gave up any hope that the young woman was going to be of any use, reaching for the phone that would connect her to the staffroom just along the corridor.

'Jenny!' she said gratefully when she recognised her voice, knowing that the staff nurse was a far better bet in an emergency than man-obsessed Julia. 'I need you in the nursery, quickly. Can you come in here and keep an eye on Adam for me? I need to get Rani up to MRI.'

'Hey, you can't just grab a baby and use it as an excuse to dash off after a doctor,' Julia objected, but Nadia simply ignored her, her hands moving in a blur to get everything ready as soon as possible.

'What's up?' Jenny demanded, pulling disposable gloves on as she entered the nursery.

'Can you phone up to MRI and tell them I'm on my way with Rani?' she directed as she took the brake off Rani's cot and began to push it towards the door. 'Then try to calm Adam down so he doesn't make himself sick.'

That was one of the drawbacks when their patients finally had the ventilator tubes taken out of their mouths, she mused, desperately trying not to think that she might be making a monumental fool of herself. For as long as they were in position, their charges were unable to use their vocal cords, and it almost seemed as if they were making up for lost time once they *were* able to.

'Nadia. What happened?' Josh demanded as he met her at the door to the room housing the massive bulk of the MRI.

'I think there's been a mix-up,' she gasped, winded from her rapid journey. 'I think some of the samples were confused and it's *Rani* who has NEC.'

'That's impossible!' he denied immediately, clearly stung by the idea that something so basic and so potentially life-threatening could have gone wrong in his department.

'I'm sorry,' Nadia said, wondering if the next few seconds would result in her losing her job before she could even hand in her resignation. She was overwhelmingly aware that Gideon was standing right behind her, listening to every word, and really didn't want his last memory of her being one of leaping to crazy conclusions on insufficient evidence. 'But if a relatively new member of staff didn't label the samples properly, and was responsible for delivering two sets of samples to the lab at the same time, isn't it possible that there might have been a mix-up?'

Josh made no comment, but his dark glower didn't need words as he strode across to place an urgent call to the labs.

'In the meantime,' he continued almost before the receiver hit the cradle at the end of a very terse conversation, 'we'll be scanning both babies, just to make sure.'

'Shall I return to the unit, then?' Nadia asked, still not certain whether she'd redeemed herself but absolutely certain that the nurse who'd made the mistakes would be receiving a reprimand…at the very least.

'Who's looking after Adam?' Gideon demanded, recalling the reason she hadn't come with Amy in the first place.

'Jenny Barber's keeping him company for me till I get back,' she told him as soothingly as possible. He had enough stress to cope with, worrying about Amy. He didn't need to be concerned about Adam, too, so she tried to put his mind at ease. 'Jenny's the slender one with the dark auburn hair and she's very good with the babies, so he's in good hands.'

With Josh standing there with a dark glower on his face, it was no wonder that both Amy and Rani were swiftly scanned.

It was only when they were positioned one after the other in the maw of the MRI that it became painfully obvious just how small they were and there was little satisfaction for Nadia when the extent of Rani's problem was revealed, even though she was as delighted as Gideon to see that Amy was completely clear of any sign of NEC.

The phone call from the lab that greeted them on their return to the unit was welcome confirmation that there was no obviously sinister reason for Amy's sudden rise in temperature, but by that time Josh was already involved in making rapid arrangements for Rani to be taken to Theatre.

'You both look shattered,' Jenny said when Amy was settled back in the cot with Adam, who'd instantly fallen into a peaceful sleep as if he hadn't just fretted for more than an hour while she was away. 'I don't mind keeping an eye on the two of them for a while if you want to get a cup of coffee. You look as if you need it.'

'I definitely need something,' Gideon agreed, 'although I'm not certain that coffee's going to be strong enough.'

'Well, I'm afraid that's all that's on offer here,' Nadia said as she led the way along the corridor. 'If you want anything stronger, you'll have to wait till you get home.'

'I don't think I dare to leave the hospital yet,' he admitted wearily. 'That was almost worse than when they were newborn.'

'Why?' Nadia had an idea she knew what he meant, but he probably needed to get his thoughts out into the open if he was going to regain the confidence to leave his precious babies in her care.

'Well, *then* they were so small and fragile that it was almost a foregone conclusion that they were going to die sooner or later. It just felt as if I had to be here for every second of their lives because they were going to be that short.'

'And, now?' she prompted.

'Now they aren't just two nondescript pathetic little scraps hanging on to life by their fingernails.' He spoke slowly, as though he was having to dredge the words from somewhere deep inside where he hid his most private emotions.

'Now they're two tiny people with individual identities,' he continued with a ghost of a smile curving that mouth that looked as if it had been made for smiling, 'We've been through so many things together over the last few weeks and it had finally begun to look as if we were winning, and suddenly...' He shook his head, the smile gone, and she could see the residual fear lurking in his eyes while the words began to pour out of him in a torrent. 'Suddenly it felt as if we were right back at the beginning again, and Amy could be taken away from me at any moment, and the thought of anyone having to operate on her when she's so tiny...'

She knew exactly how he felt because that was the way she'd been feeling, too. Her fear that Amy might die...if not from NEC then from complications due to the extent of the surgery she would need to eradicate it...couldn't have been more personal than if she was losing Anya all over again.

'But now you know she *hasn't* got it…' She searched for the most tactful way to say this. 'Can you not trust me to be there for her? With her? Can you not have the confidence that I would phone you?'

Those deep green eyes gazed into hers for so long that it felt as if he wanted to see all the way into her soul. Then he gave a single nod and closed his eyes for several weary seconds.

'Of course I trust you, Nadia,' he said softly. 'But I just…I feel so helpless to do anything for them. It would probably be easier if there was something I could do…' His words died away abruptly and a sudden spark lit his eyes.

'Breast milk!' he exclaimed. 'I remember reading something when I was doing research soon after they were born. Isn't breast milk supposed to stop them suffering from NEC?'

For such an apparently clinical subject, why did it suddenly make her feel as if she ought to be shielding her own breasts from him? This wasn't about *her*. It was about the needs of Amy and Adam.

'Statistically, it does seem to give premature babies a great deal of protection,' she agreed, seriously, 'although there's no guarantee that it will completely prevent them from developing NEC.'

'But it would be worth giving it to them, if only to…' His enthusiasm died almost as suddenly as it had leapt to life. 'Except they don't have a mother willing to give them milk…unless there's someone in the department who would be willing…' He rammed his fingers through his hair, clearly frustrated. 'As if that's going to work!' he exclaimed. 'I can hardly go up to someone and ask her to sell me a pint of milk…as if she were a dairy cow, or something!'

Nadia chuckled at the image that conjured up inside her head. 'No. You couldn't. But there is always the milk bank.'

'Milk bank?' he repeated, his tired brain apparently having trouble with understanding the term, although she was sure he must have read about it. 'Is that like the blood bank?'

'Very similar,' she agreed. 'Lactating mothers express their spare milk so that it's available for babies with allergy problems, or for premature babies like Amy and Adam. Obviously, there are safeguards in place— the mother has a blood test and must be a non-smoker and drugs free, and the milk she donates is frozen before being sent off to be thoroughly checked and pasteurised before it can be used for another baby.'

'And this is readily available?'

'Because breast milk is so much better for babies than any formula, it is something we have often taken advantage of, when the natural mother can't or isn't willing to provide the milk herself.' Why on earth was she feeling so uncomfortable talking about this? It was a discussion she must have had with dozens of parents since she'd started working in the unit. There was nothing personal—

'Would you be willing to do it?' he asked suddenly, and for a moment she was speechless, her brain trying to work out what he was saying even as her heart ached with the memories of all the fledgling plans she'd started to weave for her own child in those few precious weeks before…

'You mean, would I be willing to provide milk for

other babies?' she asked, firmly shutting those painful
images in the smallest, darkest corner of her mind.
Before he could reply, she added quickly. 'That would
depend, of course, on whether I'd recently had a child
of my own, whether I was going to feed it myself and
whether I had a surplus of milk.'

'But you would want to feed your own child,' he said
softly. 'And if you had spare milk, you'd willingly offer
it to other babies who needed it,' he added, his voice
filled with the same certainty that she could see in that
serious green gaze. Her heart swelled at the thought
that he could know her so well.

CHAPTER SEVEN

GIDEON slumped into the last remaining comfortable chair, almost slopping his coffee over his knee before his seat hit the rather saggy upholstery.

'I hate Friday and Saturday nights,' grumbled one of the nurses as she shouldered her way into the room in his wake.

'It's the drunks that I hate,' Gideon said. 'I've lost count of how many we've had tonight.'

'Tell me about it!' she exclaimed as she filled the kettle. 'Gangs of drunken yobs shouting the odds and thinking they can bully us into doing what they want just because they're bigger and heavier than we are. Thank goodness the hospital's put some security measures in place. At least we don't get attacked quite so often any more.'

Gideon was glad about that, because he'd been one of the people who'd argued strongly for having armed guards on the premises. When they were dealing with the results of gangs and drugs, it was only fair the staff that they should have appropriate protection in place.

When they were being abusive, it could be hard to remember that drunken patients sometimes needed even more care than sober ones. The overwhelming smell of

alcohol could disguise the fact that the patient was unconscious due to injuries rather than drink.

'Drunken adults is one thing, but it's the youngsters
who really get to me,' he admitted darkly, staring into
his coffee.

Specifically, the underage teenagers who should
have been safely at home with their parents, not out in
the pubs and clubs getting so drunk that the para-
medics were having to scoop their unconscious bodies
out of the gutters to bring them in to have their
stomachs pumped.

And for some the alcohol was the least of their
problems. Like that last patient he'd seen...the one that
had sent him in here for a much-needed break. The
pretty young girl whose body had been found dumped
in the alley behind one of the clubs, surrounded by
refuse and showing obvious signs that she'd been raped,
repeatedly, while she'd been too drunk to defend herself.

'Oh,' she murmured with sudden understanding.
'You were the one who had to deal with that girl they
brought in. Is she...is she going to be all right?'

Gideon closed his eyes but there was nothing he
could do to get rid of the image of that youngster. She'd
looked like a broken doll as she'd lain there on the table,
and there had been absolutely nothing he'd been able to
do to save her from the effects of the drugs and alcohol
in her body. The fact that she'd been physically abused,
too, had almost been irrelevant as he'd fought to stop
her organs shutting down.

'No, she's not,' he said, and his voice felt like gravel
in his throat. 'By the time her parents arrived, she was
dead. And they hadn't even known she was going out.

They thought she was staying with a school friend to watch videos or something.'

Unfortunately, he knew that the devastation on the couple's faces would fade from his memory far too quickly, replaced by other equally harrowing events.

No wonder so many A and E staff suffered from burn-out. It was either that, or allow themselves to become totally hardened to what they were seeing and doing, and that was a route he didn't want to take.

He sighed, and tried to put the events of the night out of his mind, concentrating instead on his recent conversation with Nadia.

She'd already organised for both Amy and Adam to receive donated breast milk, and he was grateful for the fact that she'd known so much about the system the hospital had in place. But it was Nadia herself, and in particular her reaction to the topic, that seemed to be stuck in his brain.

He had no idea what had prompted him to ask if she intended to breastfeed her own children, but once the words had left his mouth all he could think about was how perfect a picture it would make to see her cradling a baby to her while it suckled. His body had, of course, had a predictably male reaction to the image of her naked breasts, but it had been her unexpected sadness that had struck him.

And the more he thought about it, the more he was coming to believe that her calm sweetness hid depths of sorrow that she would not easily speak about.

The hospital grapevine being what it was, he already knew that she lived alone, but no one seemed to know any more than that—certainly not something as personal as whether she'd ever had a relationship that had resulted in a pregnancy, or even in a child who was no longer with her.

He couldn't imagine that the woman who cared for his two babies with such fierce dedication would ever have abandoned a child of her own, but something devastating had definitely caused her to shut down, and, while he wanted to know what it was, more than anything he wanted her to trust him enough to tell him about it.

The sound of raised voices outside the dubious solitude of his refuge dragged him away from his speculations and back to the fact that he still had far too many hours left to his shift before he could escape to the relative peace of the unit upstairs. Ever since Adam and Amy's early arrival in the world, his entire focus had shifted so that the two of them were at the heart of his day. Every time he had to leave them, he couldn't wait until he could be with them again, and whereas at first the feeling had been one of desperation…that every minute with them might be their last…he was slowly beginning to believe that his time with them, was just the start of a whole lifetime.

And the fact that there was an extra eagerness in his step whenever he took the stairs up to the unit with the knowledge that he would be seeing Nadia again…well, that was something he would have to keep to himself.

'Once more into the breach, dear friends…' he quoted fatalistically, then downed the last of his coffee and forced himself to his feet. 'It sounds as if the next wave of the flotsam and jetsam of Friday night's humanity has been washed to our door. It's a good thing we like our jobs.'

* * *

Nadia resisted the urge to look over her shoulder as she hurried towards the welcoming entrance of A and E.

For more than a week now she'd had the uncomfortably prickly sensation on the back of her neck that someone was watching her and, as much as she'd tried to convince herself that it was all in her imagination, the feeling scared her.

It wasn't that the hospital grounds were poorly lit, because they weren't. Since a spate of muggings a couple of years ago the security was almost as stringent in the surrounding paths and car parks as it was in the hospital itself, with newly installed lighting making everywhere almost as bright as daylight no matter what time it was.

No, there were very few shadows large enough to hide a potential assailant, but that didn't mean that there couldn't be someone hiding in plain sight, mingling with the constant flow of people moving in and out of what was the main entrance to the hospital. If someone wanted to keep an eye on her and track her comings and goings, it would be all too easy for him to duck behind a group of patients or visitors, or even to walk beside them and strike up a conversation so that he seemed to belong.

She could all too easily imagine Laszlo doing such a thing. He'd certainly had enough practice at pretending to be invisible, and just the thought that he might be spying on her while he made his plans was enough to make her shake in her sensible shoes.

She blew out a breath of relief when the automatic doors slid closed behind her and tried to shrug off the creepy sensation as she made her way swiftly towards the corridor leading to the staffroom.

If she was logical about it, she would dismiss the person she'd seen as someone who only bore a passing resemblance to the man who had destroyed her innocent dreams. The terror that had dominated every second of her day when she'd first escaped was in the past now. She was a very different person from that pathetic girl; someone with a profession and a future she could be proud of; someone with colleagues who respected her and with friends who would help her if she were to ask.

She tapped on the door and pushed it open just far enough to put her head through to see if Gideon was there, suddenly unaccountably shy.

For the first time since she'd been a daydreaming teenager with pictures of actors and singers on her walls, in the days when the world had still seemed an exciting place full of endless possibilities, she found herself daring to hope that she might have found the one man who could restore her faith in the goodness of men.

The prospect was scary, because for there to be a chance for something *more* to develop between them, she would have to be prepared to tell him about the events of her past...and she didn't know if she would ever be brave enough to do that. She couldn't bear it if she were to see the welcoming smile in those beautiful green eyes turn to cold disgust.

Would it be better if she were to keep a professional distance between them? Could she allow the tentative friendship that seemed to be developing, even though she was beginning to wonder if that would ever be enough to fill the emptiness inside her.

'Nadia! Come in! Would you prefer tea or coffee?'

The warmth in Gideon's voice and in his smile was

irresistible, and her determination to just hand over the package in her hand and go straight up to the unit melted without trace.

'You mentioned that you like gingerbread,' she said diffidently as she handed over her little burden. 'I've never made it before, but I found a recipe that—'

'Mmm!' he groaned as he sank his teeth into the first dark golden brown square, and to her amazement her body reacted to the sexy sound almost as though it could feel his pleasure.

'That is just so…' He bit off another large mouthful and closed his eyes as he chewed, his expression one of obvious ecstasy. His thick dark lashes flicked up to reveal gleaming green eyes. 'This is the best gingerbread I've ever eaten,' he said fervently. 'And you say it's the first time you've ever made it?'

She nodded, delighted that he was enjoying her offering. She'd never particularly enjoyed cooking when it had been a daily chore trying to stretch what little her family had to feed all those mouths. And since her betrayal, she'd never once cooked any dish that reminded her of that dreadful time.

Anyway, she'd rather make something that Gideon enjoyed. That way, it seemed worth the effort, where cooking for one never really did.

'Aren't you having any?' he asked a few moments later when he handed her the coffee she'd requested. 'Don't you like it?'

'I've never had it before,' she admitted. 'I wasn't sure if that was the way it was supposed to taste, or if I'd put too much ginger in.'

'Ooh! That smells good!' exclaimed one of Gideon's

young male colleagues as he refilled the kettle. 'Any going spare?'

'Not really,' Gideon said with a grimace as he wrapped the foil firmly around the remaining pieces. 'It was Nadia's first attempt and she's put far too much ginger in. Perhaps you'll be able to have some when she gets the recipe right.'

'Oh. That's a shame,' he said with a shrug as the criticism made Nadia's heart sink.

Had she really made a big mistake with her measurements of the ingredients? She'd only tasted the crumbs as she'd cut it up to bring to the hospital, and it hadn't seemed too spicy to her, but perhaps—

'Take it up to the unit,' Gideon muttered under his breath as he pressed the misshapen parcel into her hands. 'James is a gannet if there's any food around, and this is far too good to waste on him.' His wink sent her emotions soaring, especially when he added, 'We can share the rest when I come up to the unit.'

Her spirits were so high at the prospect of seeing him again later that she'd all but forgotten the uncomfortable sensation that she was being watched until she emerged into the reception area of A and E to make her way to the stairs that would take her to the unit to start her shift.

Suddenly, it was back with a vengeance, and this time the impression was so strong that it almost felt as if the watcher was standing right behind her.

Nadia froze with her hand on the door, desperate to escape the feeling of menace, but something drew her away from the potential isolation of a largely empty stairwell. If anyone *was* following her, it would be all too easy for her to be trapped out of the sight of anyone who could help.

She paused just long enough to take stock of her options then deliberately waited until the doors of the nearest lift were starting to close on nearly a dozen occupants before hurrying into it at the last second.

Feeling like an animal that had just escaped from the jaws of a trap, she drew in a shaky breath while she concentrated on watching the numbers flick past one by one.

The lift stopped twice to let some of the occupants get off and others get on and each time she found herself holding her breath, terrified that Laszlo was going to be the next passenger to get on.

She was shaking like a leaf by the time the door to the unit closed behind her and she knew that she was safe. To minimise the chance of importing infections from the rest of the hospital to some of its most vulnerable patients, the security in this part of the department was so strict that only those who knew the door code could enter, and that meant that this was one place where Laszlo couldn't follow her.

Not that the security stopped her from feeling jumpy, though. It seemed that every five minutes someone was stopping behind her on silent feet and nearly making her jump out of her skin when they spoke. The only difference when it was Gideon who startled her was that he was the only one who made her want to leap into his arms. And if that wasn't crazy, then nothing was.

'What's the matter?' he demanded after one glance at her face. 'Has something happened to Adam and Amy?'

'No!' she exclaimed, silently castigating herself for giving him even a moment's unnecessary worry. 'In fact, just the opposite—they've both put on some weight. Not a lot and not as much as we would have hoped by now, but at least the trend is in the right direction.'

She'd never known a set of twins so closely in tune with each other. It seemed almost as if one of them couldn't put on weight unless the other did, so with the various setbacks they'd each suffered they'd been slow to make any headway towards the target they'd have to reach before it was safe to let them 'graduate' from the humidicrib.

So far, they'd been lucky that there hadn't been any more desperately sick babies needing the intensive care that the unit could provide. She couldn't imagine how she would feel if the two of them had to be transferred to someone else's care before she was certain that they were out of danger.

Come to that, she couldn't imagine how she was going to feel when the two of them were ready to go home. There was going to be the most enormous void in her life once they…and Gideon…were no longer a part of it.

'Nadia?' There was an unfamiliar hesitancy to Gideon's voice that immediately caught her attention. 'Do you think…? Would you like…?'

He gave a huff of annoyance when he couldn't seem to find the words he wanted and there was an endearing hint of colour in his cheeks that made her wonder what on earth he was trying to say.

'Would you think it inappropriate if I were to ask you to share a meal with me?' The question almost burst out of him and for just one wonderful moment she allowed the pleasure to flood through her.

Gideon was asking her out! He wanted to take her for a meal!

She felt her eyes widen and was sure she must have a grin stretching from one ear to the other.

'I know a meal would never be enough to say thank you for all your care of Adam and Amy,' he continued, clearly uncomfortable, and the realisation that the invitation was nothing more than a demonstration of gratitude was like a bucket of cold water being thrown over her.

'You don't have to do that,' she interrupted, her voice sharpened by disappointment. Taking care of babies like Amy and Adam was her job and she didn't need empty gestures for doing what she loved. Her reward was to see them thrive and—

'But,' he continued in a rush, apparently oblivious to the fact that she'd spoken 'the truth is, I'd rather like to spend some time with you away from the hospital… away from the unit and A and E.'

That declaration was such a shock that she just stood there staring at him with her mouth open.

Had he actually said that he wanted to spend time with her? Was he really asking her out? Her? Nadia Pirz…Nadia *Smith*? She corrected herself hastily, horrified that so many years of hiding behind her new name could be undone in a matter of seconds when her emotions were scrambled by an invitation from a tall dark green-eyed man.

Thank goodness he couldn't read her thoughts or she was certain that keen brain of his would have come up with an inexhaustible supply of questions, and she couldn't risk that, not if Laszlo was lurking around.

'Thank you very much for the invitation,' she managed through a throat strangled by disappointment, but he beamed.

'Tomorrow evening?' he asked eagerly, before she

had a chance to finish, and it nearly broke her heart to continue with what she had to say.

'You're very kind to invite me, but I'm afraid it just isn't possible,' she said, hearing just how stilted she sounded, even though her pulse seemed to echo strangely in her ears.

Oh, she wanted *so* much to accept, to spend some time with the only man who'd ever made her think that she might one day be able to respond as if she were a normal woman. She would love to sit at a table with him, sharing a leisurely meal while they shared the sort of conversation that would let the two of them get to know each other outside the hospital setting that had dominated their relationship so far.

Relationship? What relationship? mocked a little voice inside her head. *If he knew who you really were, where you came from, what you've done...do you think he'd be inviting you out for a meal? Ha! He wouldn't let you near his babies for another second, and as for sharing a meal...!*

'You'd be safe,' he said earnestly, and for one awful moment she wondered if her brain was so scrambled that she'd actually said something aloud about Laszlo. 'I was only going to suggest we went to that little Italian restaurant just off the high street. It's family owned and all the recipes have been handed down from the grand-mother to her daughter-in-law and the atmosphere is very relaxed and friendly.'

'I'm sure it's lovely, but I'm sorry. I can't,' she said, knowing exactly which place he was talking about. She gazed longingly at the menu every time she walked past but had known that she could never go there by herself.

She would feel far too conspicuous, being the only single woman in a restaurant full of couples, and the last thing she ever wanted was to draw attention to herself.

Especially now.

There was a slightly strained atmosphere between the two of them for the rest of the evening, in spite of the fact that he'd apparently accepted her refusal with equanimity, and it was only when he was sitting with both babies cradled in his arms that the matter seemed finally to be forgotten.

'When I remember how desperately tiny they were the first time I saw them, I can see just how much they've grown,' he mused in a gentle voice, careful not to overload their fragile auditory systems. She glanced up at him from her careful cleaning procedure and was flustered to find that he was looking at her rather than the babies.

'I can remember when you measured the top joint of your thumb against Adam's foot and they were the same size,' Nadia said, hoping to deflect his attention back to his son and daughter. It had been years since she'd been comfortable having anyone looking at her too closely. 'You can actually see that there's a difference now.'

'But then today in A and E I saw a full-term baby that was born the same week as Adam and Amy, and he seemed absolutely *huge* in comparison to them, even though he didn't have a particularly high birth weight.'

'We get so accustomed to seeing really tiny babies that it's easy to forget the size they *should* be before they're ready to face the world.' She'd finished the chores that had given Gideon the excuse to have an extra cuddle with the two of them, but he looked so *right* sitting there with them that she stood for several moments just enjoying the picture they made. She had absolutely no doubt that he was going to be a good father to them, and the realisation that she wouldn't be there to see it happen on a day-to-day basis was enough to bring tears to her eyes.

Gideon stayed a while longer after Adam and Amy had been settled back into the cot and had fallen asleep immediately, apparently exhausted by the excitement of their outing.

He seemed pensive, his thoughts obviously else-where even though his gaze rarely strayed far from the peaceful scene in front of him.

Suddenly he straightened up out of the torture of the moulded plastic seat with an air of decision.

'I'll be back later,' he announced briskly, already be-ginning to strip off his disposable gloves and apron, and she was left almost stunned by his sudden departure.

The good thing about his absence was that it gave her time to mourn her decision not to accept his invitation. It had been so hard stopping herself from telling him that she'd changed her mind, but the more she thought about it, the more she knew that she'd made the right decision.

If she'd just been Nadia Smith, the specialist nurse who'd been taking care of his babies, she would have been delighted to accept, even if the invitation had been nothing more than Gideon's way of saying thank you. But she was Nadia Smith with secrets in her past— secrets that, if they had caught up with her, could put Gideon in danger.

'Ha! That's an understatement,' she muttered, knowing only too well what Laszlo was capable of. And until she knew one way or the other whether it was her nemesis who was making her flesh crawl every time she left the shelter of the hospital building, she hardly dared to be seen in Gideon's company, let alone accept an invitation to go somewhere public with him.

Even though she was kept busy, the time seemed almost to drag now that Gideon wasn't there, and it was a relief when she glanced at the clock to realise that it was almost time for her meal break.

'Hey, Nadia. Ready to go?' asked Jenny a few minutes later as she came into the nursery, pulling on fresh disposable gloves as she approached the humidi-crib. 'I hope you've told these two to behave themselves while you're gone.'

The conversation was similar to one they'd had on many occasions since the younger nurse had joined the unit, but there was something about the russet-haired nurse that was different today. There was an air of... almost suppressed excitement, an extra sparkle to her eyes as if she was hiding a delicious secret.

'Oh, drat!' she exclaimed, almost too casually as she leaned forward to read the latest notations on the babies' charts, and Nadia's antennae started to twitch. 'I left my coffee-mug on the desk outside. Could you drop it off in the staff lounge before you go down for your meal? Thanks.'

The warning signal was almost an audible buzz by the time she reached the door to the staff lounge, courtesy of at least one hastily smothered grin and a whispered conversation that was rapidly terminated as she walked past.

The reason for the electric atmosphere only became

clear when she opened the door and found Gideon waiting for her with a full carrier bag that was filling the room with delicious aromas.

'You wouldn't agree to come out for a meal, so I brought the meal to you,' he announced, then spoiled the whole announcement by asking uncertainly, 'I hope you don't mind?'

Nadia didn't know whether to be delighted or to tell him off. This certainly wasn't the way to keep a low profile, and if the hospital grapevine got hold of what had gone on this evening, that would make it all the more likely that Laszlo would get to hear about it.

But…

'Oh, Gideon.' How could she help but feel flattered that he had gone to so much trouble for her?

'If her Ladyship would care to take a seat?' He made a gesture towards the settee, then started to unload the goodies from the enormous insulated bag he'd placed on the low table in front of it.

Uncertainly, she stepped forward to settle herself on the slightly battered cushions, suddenly realising that this was the first time she'd ever been brought a meal by a man.

Ever since she'd escaped from Laszlo, she'd been careful not to put herself in the position where she would have to turn down invitations…until Gideon had come along. Somehow there was something about this man that was slowly but steadily demolishing every one of the barriers she'd erected against risking the sort of pain she'd gone through at the hands of men.

Perhaps it was the fact that, even when he was at his most stressed and most exhausted, he'd never once raised his voice and, although he'd been incredibly stubborn about staying at his babies' side, she couldn't help but be impressed at his devotion to them, even at the expense of his own health.

This, she knew with utter certainty, wasn't a man who would raise his hand against a woman, and that very certainty was the thing that allowed her to look up into his waiting green eyes and smile from her heart.

'Gideon, you shouldn't have done this, but thank you,' she said round the lump in her throat. 'No one's ever done anything this special for me.'

'You don't know what special is until you've tasted this food,' he said with a grin. 'Prepare to be amazed.'

CHAPTER EIGHT

NADIA'S break was only half an hour, and most of the time was spent in eating the wonderful selection of dishes he'd brought for her to taste.

'Now you'll know what to order when we go there,' he said with a twinkle in his eye as he collected the empty containers while she ran hot water into the sink to wash the plates and cutlery.

Her heart gave an extra thump at the thought that he was already planning for them to eat together again.

'Oh, Gideon…it's not that I didn't want to go for a meal with you,' she heard herself say, her tongue obviously loosened by the good food and the relaxed atmosphere between them. 'It's just…it isn't a very good idea to draw attention like this.'

He stopped in mid-stride, an arrested expression on his face.

'You're not married, are you?' he demanded, and for just a moment her mind went back to the day she'd believed she *was* getting married. It had been too late when she'd discovered that it had been nothing more than a sham.

'No, I'm not married,' she confirmed, saddened by

the look of obvious relief on his face because, some time soon, she was going to have to tell him that there was no chance of anything more than a temporary friendship between them, certainly nothing as permanent as marriage. It was already more than she'd ever hoped for to spend even this much time in his company.

'You already know that I was married,' he said wryly, and she remembered her blunder in suggesting that he should go up to visit his wife.

'Are you still in love with her?' she asked, even as she realised that it was a totally inappropriate question. What business was it of hers what his feelings were for his ex-wife?

'Not any more.' His voice was quiet but firm, his green gaze steady. 'In the end I think it was all the procedures that killed it for us. When we stopped making love and just…well, mated to try to give her the baby she wanted, all spontaneity was destroyed by charts and thermometers.'

He shook his head and she could see the sadness that the memories put in his eyes. 'When the months went past, she decided that IVF would be the answer, but so much of that process is so clinical…so impersonal…so downright invasive that it doesn't matter how good the doctors and nurses are, the strain gradually builds up…especially when month after month you're almost holding your breath that *this* time it's finally worked… Only it never did.'

There was a tap at the door while Nadia was still trying to find words to convey her sympathy.

'I'm so sorry to interrupt,' said a voice on the other side of the door, and a head poked round with an apologetic expression, 'but Jenny would like you to come into the nursery. She's not happy with something on one of the monitors.'

Immediately, the two of them whirled away from each other to make their way as swiftly as possible into the nursery, and Nadia found herself resenting the time it took to use the hand gel and don apron and gloves.

In the end it turned out to be nothing more than a false alarm, caused by Adam tugging on a lead and disturbing one of Amy's sensors just enough to set it off.

'If you keep doing that, young man, we're going to have to move you to separate cots,' Nadia warned, her heart taking longer than she would have liked to return to its normal rhythm with all that adrenaline circulating through her system.

'Were going to have to separate them sooner rather than later,' Gideon pointed out. 'They're small enough to share at the moment, but it won't be long until they need more space. And then they'll *have* to get accustomed to the idea that they aren't close enough to touch each other all the time.'

'But not yet,' Nadia said quickly, even as her brain wondered what it would be like to have someone she loved close enough to touch in the dark loneliness of the night…as if *that* was ever going to happen. After what she'd gone through at Laszlo's hands, it was still a struggle for her to share a lift with strangers. Whether she would ever be able to bring herself to trust a man to share her bed…

'Coward!' Gideon taunted, and for one heartstopping moment she thought he'd been reading her mind. 'You just don't want to have to put up with the crying when they're separated. You want *me* to have to suffer it when I take them home.'

'I don't think that's likely,' she said in all seriousness. 'They're both still on oxygen, but if everything goes well, they'll soon be strong enough to graduate from the nursery here to the normal paediatric area until they're finally ready for release. Probably that's where they'll try to wean them off their dependence on each other... before you take them home.'

And talking to him about the usual progression of premature babies through the unit was as close as she wanted to come to thinking about the day he and his little family would finally leave.

Even so, at the end of her shift she paused outside the department while she tried to decide between the adult thing to do...taking the lift that would deliver her to the nearest exit to make her way home...or walking to the other end of the department so that she would make her way down through A and E, just on the off-chance that she might catch a glimpse of Gideon at the start of his next shift.

'Excuse me,' she said to the slightly harried-looking man loitering in the corridor outside the unit, blocking her access to the lifts.

She wondered briefly why he was there. If his wife was having a baby, there was a designated waiting area where he could pace, if he didn't want to go into the delivery room with her.

Then a melodic chime announced the lift's arrival and she still hadn't made up her mind...or had she? Was there any doubt that she was going to go the longer way, through Gideon's domain?

She knew she was being stupid, and was undoubtedly setting herself up for a hefty dose of heartache when Amy, Adam and their father were no longer part of her life, but there was something so liberating about reverting to the teenager she'd almost forgotten existed, the memories buried under a landslide of horror that had destroyed her innocence for ever.

Her heart leapt into her throat, beating like a rabbit's as terror overtook her, and her feet felt as if they were nailed to the floor as she caught sight of the man who looked so similar to Laszlo again.

This time there was no cowed and frightened girl with him. He just seemed to be idly leaning against the wall, out of the way of all the passing traffic but with his eyes never still as they flickered over the face of each new person who entered the reception area.

At the very last second her survival instincts kicked in and she backed swiftly into the gaping entrance of the lift to huddle out of sight in the furthest corner, where he wouldn't be able to see her.

Was it him? Had he caught sight of her?

If it *was* him, was her disguise so poor that he'd recognised her the other day? She'd thought that changing her name, her hair colour and style and her eye colour would have been sufficient to keep her safe, but had he seen straight through it? Was he only waiting for a chance to force her to repay him the money he was owed?

She pressed the button repeatedly and finally the doors began to swish closed even as she heard heavy feet approaching. She didn't dare to peer around the entrance to see who wanted to join her in the isolation of the brushed-steel box. She was too terrified that it was Laszlo. If he got into the lift with her...

At the very last second she saw a hand—a male hand—reaching out towards the rapidly closing gap between the doors and whimpered with relief when it failed to stop them shutting him out.

To her horror, the lift barely began its ascent when it slowed for the next floor.

She was trembling from head to foot by the time the doors began to slide open, revealing several members of staff surrounding a gurney filled with a large patient and an enormous amount of life-support equipment.

'Excuse me,' she whispered, suddenly aware that it could take several minutes for them to get themselves organised in the limited space...time she couldn't afford to waste if Laszlo was on his way.

Fear lent wings to her feet as she sped along the corridor to the next bank of lifts, deliberately ignoring the training that told her to 'walk briskly without running'.

It felt as if it took for ever, but it couldn't have been many minutes before she was outside the main hospital building and hurrying to lose herself in the anonymity of the people thronging the pavement.

Once inside her little bed sit she threw the door bolts top and bottom and turned both keys, but still didn't feel safe.

If she was honest with herself, she'd known that renting a room on the ground floor had never been a good idea, but she hadn't been able to resist the fact that she could look out on the tiny patch of garden that had been filled with spring blossoms the first time she'd seen it. Now she was overwhelmingly aware of just how vulnerable she would be to someone determined to get in.

Not that she had much worth stealing…just the bare minimum of clothing in a tiny space that boasted nothing more than the most basic furniture. Even so, she found herself reaching for the soft-sided bag on top of her wardrobe and systematically folding and packing everything that she couldn't bear to leave behind just in case it was Laszlo and she had to leave.

Her hand hovered briefly over the loose floorboard that hid the cash she'd squirrelled away whenever she could, but she left it there for the time being, concentrating on her task as she spread the rest of the hangers out in the wardrobe to make the fact that she'd taken a number of items out look less obvious. She did the same in the chest of drawers, just taking enough underwear and essentials for survival, knowing that if she did have to leave in a hurry, she probably wouldn't want to be carrying anything too heavy.

Nerves made it difficult to eat, even though she knew the importance of giving her body the fuel it needed to be strong, and fear made it almost impossible to sleep, her eyes flicking open with every sudden sound, her heart pounding until she identified the source and subsided back onto the pillow.

Nadia was absolutely exhausted by the time she was due to leave for work next morning, and sad beyond belief that she would have to leave the hospital before Amy and Adam were strong enough to go home. She didn't want to go—just the thought of it was breaking her heart. But there was no way that she could allow Laszlo to take her back to the existence she'd only just escaped with her life.

She waited nervously for the lift, glad that there was someone else waiting with her until she saw the same man she'd bumped into as she'd been leaving the department the previous day. He looked almost as dreadful as she felt, and she wondered if his wife was having a particularly difficult labour.

Hopefully, it wouldn't result in a baby that needed a place in the unit. When she left, it would leave them very short of specialist staff, especially if someone else was taken ill.

She should really have phoned in this morning, making an excuse not to come to work at all, but she couldn't make herself do it. Her colleagues deserved better, as did her patients, and she couldn't bear to just leave. After all, it might not even have been Laszlo.

Worry that she was taking a risk by not running while she had a chance, guilt at the fact that she would be abandoning her little charges was also mixed with anger that the situation was being forced on her, but she was too exhausted to maintain either emotion. All she really cared about was spending as much time as possible with Amy and Adam, and with Gideon when he arrived at the end of his shift.

No, she wasn't going to think about Gideon, or she would have to admit just how much he had come to mean to her, in spite of the fact that there was absolutely no possibility that they could ever be together.

The red phone rang just five minutes before Gideon was due to finish his shift and the information that the ambulance crew was bringing in a paediatric arrest wouldn't let him leave, no matter how his heart sank.

The baby was mottled and blue as the paramedic strode in, carrying it, and the paediatric resuscitation team that the senior nurse had called down arrived on the scene almost unheard over the distraught mother's screaming.

Unfortunately, this was a well-practised drill, and every member of the team started to perform their part of the resuscitation attempt in spite of the fact that they all knew the probable outcome. This was obviously a cot death and they would go through the motions just in case the baby could be revived, but their efforts were more for the sake of the parents, so that they could be certain while they grieved that everything possible had been done to bring their child back to them.

'He's six months old,' murmured one of the team, but he didn't look up. They all had their parts to play and as the baby's heart had stopped beating so long ago that there was no possibility of finding a vein, his job was to get an interosseous line into the bone in his little blue leg so that fluids could be administered.

The needle looked big and ugly and Gideon felt queasy when he felt the sudden pop that told him he'd positioned it correctly, glad that he wasn't the paediatric registrar in charge of directing all this effort. He'd done his part, hooking up the fluids and administering the drugs that had been drawn up ready for him, but all he could think of was the fact that Adam and Amy were even more vulnerable than this baby. It was all too easy to imagine himself standing there like those desperate parents while something similar was done to one of his babies.

The child looked like a rag doll as the chest compressions continued inexorably, the warning sound of the monitors and the mother's hysterical tears so heartrending that he just wanted to shout at everyone to stop and leave the tiny child with at least some dignity. Nobody wanted to be the one to utter the dreadful final words in front of his mother, but surely they had done enough to prove that he wasn't coming back?

'Stop!' someone shouted, and for an awful moment he wondered if it was him. 'Please, just stop it. Stop it,' the baby's mother sobbed as she suddenly rushed forward and began pushing them away from her child. 'Don't hurt him any more.'

No one had the heart to point out that he was beyond feeling pain, but Gideon was aware of an overwhelming feeling of relief when the paediatric registrar nodded and they could begin to remove all the monitors and lines they'd put in just twenty minutes ago.

As if he was watching something through sound-proof glass, Gideon saw the senior nurse wrap his little body in the pretty blanket that had somehow survived the journey with him, and handed him to his mother.

'Oh, sweetheart, I'm so sorry...so sorry,' she wailed as she hugged him to her chest and rocked him, and Gideon knew he couldn't stay in the room a moment longer.

There was nothing more he could do and it was already beyond the end of his shift. The only place he wanted to be was up in the nursery with his own precious babies.

'What is the matter?' Nadia demanded, and Gideon suddenly realised that he must have been staring at Adam and Amy in silence for some long while.

For a moment he contemplated shrugging the question off, the way he had during his marriage, but then realised that Nadia was nothing like Norah. She would actually understand how recent events were affecting him.

'We had a cot death come in, right at the end of the shift,' he said, remembering to keep his voice low enough that the other adults in the nursery couldn't hear their conversation. Parents dealing with babies with such a tenuous hold on life didn't need to hear about others who had lost that hold.

'You weren't able to do anything?' The way she said it told him she already knew the answer.

'He'd probably been dead for at least an hour before he was brought in,' Gideon said. 'There was no chance of resuscitation, but…'

'But you all had to look as if you were making the effort, for the sake of the parents,' she finished for him, and his heart warmed a little from its melancholy state when he realised that she *did* understand. 'How old was he?'

'Six months.' He sighed heavily. 'He was a beautiful boy, obviously well cared for and loved, and his parents…they were devastated.'

'And all you could think about was these two here,' she said, and placed a consoling hand on his arm.

Gideon froze, staring down at that innocent contact.

In all the weeks since he'd first met her, he could count on the fingers of one hand the number of times that she'd voluntarily touched him, and every time the electric sensation it caused on his skin seemed to grow stronger.

And she could feel it, too, if the way she quickly pulled her hand away was anything to go by, especially as she was now absently rubbing her palm against the side of her scrubs as though to try to wipe the sensation away.

That was something he needed to think about, as was the fact that he'd never noticed before that she wore contact lenses. He'd already noticed that she coloured her hair, but hadn't liked to mention the fact in case she was one of those people who went grey early. Actually, he found it rather endearing that a woman who seemed to care so little for high fashion and the usual feminine fripperies should take the trouble to darken her hair and get rid of the necessity for glasses.

'Have you started to make plans for taking Amy and Adam home?' Nadia asked suddenly, clearly uncomfortable with his prolonged scrutiny. 'Will you have a nanny to live in your home or will you take them to a child minder while you are at work? Or bring them to the crèche?'

As a change of direction, she couldn't have chosen anything more complicated.

'I don't know,' he admitted. It was his turn to feel uncomfortable, especially when her eyebrows rose like that.

'But it will only be weeks now before they will be ready!' she exclaimed. 'You must have some idea how you will manage.'

'When Norah and I decided to start a family, she couldn't wait to be a stay-at-home mother until the children were old enough to start school, so there was no need to think about the alternatives.' He dragged his fingers through his hair as if that might stir up a few brain cells.

She made an impatient sound. 'But once you knew that you were going to be on your own, surely you must have thought about how you were going to manage?'

'Actually, no,' he admitted with a glance down at the pair of them lying so peacefully asleep. His heart swelled with a potent mixture of fear and love. 'When they first arrived, I couldn't believe that either of them would survive long enough to come home. It still feels a bit like tempting fate, to make too many decisions. I'd rather wait until their weight gets closer to their target.'

'And then you will hope that you find the perfect solution all in a matter of days?' she challenged. 'That will not do. You must interview people to make certain that they will treat your babies the way you would want them to be treated. You must find someone you can trust with them.'

'Oh, I know the perfect person for the job,' he said with a meaningful look in her direction. 'Unfortunately, she already has a job she loves. Anyway, on an A and E doctor's salary, I wouldn't be able to afford her.'

Her eyes widened in disbelief and he was shocked to see tears well up in her eyes.

'That is a wonderful compliment,' she said huskily. 'And if things were different, I would love to be there to see the two of them grow up, but…'

'But what?' He'd been nearly as surprised to hear what had come out of his mouth as she had. He certainly hadn't intended saying anything quite so…so provocative, but now that he'd broached the idea, he couldn't seem to think about anything else. Nadia would be the perfect person to look after Adam and Amy. He only had to watch the gentle attention with which she took care of them to know that.

'But…' She hesitated a moment as though debating whether she should really speak her mind. Then, when her shoulders went back and she stared him straight in the face, he knew her decision was made. 'Gideon, what you and those babies really need is a wife to be a mother to them. That might take a little time to find, so for now you need to choose someone who will take proper care of them until you can find her.'

It was his turn to be speechless.

Whatever he'd thought she was going to say, it certainly hadn't been *that*.

'I've been married,' he pointed out when he finally managed to put two words together. 'It's not something I want to do again in a hurry.'

'Obviously that's because you weren't married to the right woman,' she fired back. 'If she was, there was no way she could have walked away from your babies, even though someone else had to carry them for you.'

Trust Nadia to put into words the disappointment he'd felt when Norah had abandoned their marriage just because she couldn't have the child she wanted.

'Childlessness affects different people in different ways,' he said in mitigation. 'She'd had her heart so set on getting pregnant that when she found it was probably never going to happen for her—'

'She didn't have enough love in her heart to give to a helpless baby, no matter who had carried it? She couldn't love that child simply because it wasn't hers?'

'Could you?' He turned her argument back on her and for just a second caught a glimpse of something gleaming in the depths of her eyes before she hid it behind a deliberate blink.

'Could *I* love a child that wasn't mine?' Her eyes betrayed her, straying towards the cot beside them for a second before she could control them, and he felt a fierce burst of exultant delight when she added, 'Of course I could.'

* * *

What was he trying to do to her?

Nadia bit her lip hard to stop the tears falling, but that didn't stop the ache in her heart.

How could Gideon have asked her if she could love a child that wasn't her own? Surely he knew that Amy and Adam meant every bit as much to her as if they had come from her own body? And the fact that they were his children only seemed to make them more precious.

And he'd used that roundabout way of saying that he wanted her to care for the two of them when it was time to take them home. At least he had no way of knowing that it was what she'd been dreaming about for weeks in the loneliness of her little room.

That was why she'd distracted him by telling him that he needed to look for a wife. She knew that even if he was able to get past the failure of his first marriage, she certainly wasn't the sort of person he could—or would—ever love, especially as she would feel honour-bound to tell him what had happened to her in the past.

The fact that she'd been stupid enough to fall in love with the man would mean nothing to him once he knew about that.

She was concentrating so hard on what was going on inside her head that she'd completely forgotten to keep her eyes open in case Laszlo was about, and when she bumped into the same man who'd been outside the lifts at the start of her shift she gave a shriek, convinced that it was Laszlo's hand gripping her arm to prevent her falling over. Or was he stopping her from running away?

'Let me go!' she pleaded, mortified to hear her voice sound as weak and pathetic as it had when she'd been sixteen.

'I'm sorry,' the man said gruffly, and immediately released her. 'I thought you were going to fall,' he added, and it was only when she registered that his accent was *pure* English that she realised it wasn't Laszlo at all.

'No. *I'm* sorry. I thought you were…someone else,' she apologised, but she was speaking to his back as he hurried away from her, almost as if couldn't bear to be near her.

Nadia could still see him making his way towards the end of the corridor and turning into the visitor's toilets as the lift doors slid closed, and she wondered idly why he was wearing such a voluminous coat when the hospital was kept so warm…and why he was walking in such an awkward, hunched way. She hadn't noticed his strange gait before, but perhaps he had some sort of injury or spinal disease? Scoliosis, perhaps?

Her eyes scanning everyone she could see once she reached the ground floor, she was making her way towards the big double doors when a burly security man suddenly stepped out in front of her, barring her exit.

'Can I ask you where you've just come from, miss?' he asked while the radio in his free hand squawked unintelligibly.

'The fourth floor,' she said, wondering what on earth was going on, especially when her answer made him frown.

'Would you mind if I were to have a look in your bag,

miss?' he asked, but she had a feeling he was going to
look whether she wanted him to or not.

'Of course I don't mind.' She held the soft cloth bag
out, holding it open wide so he could see that she had
little more than her purse and a few odds and ends in it.
With any luck he'd never notice that she had her essential papers such as her passport sewn into the lining in
the bottom. It would be difficult to explain why she
never went anywhere without them.

'I'm one of the nurses in the premature baby unit,'
she volunteered, flicking open her purse to show an ID
card. 'What are you looking for? Drugs?'

'Someone has kidnapped a baby…one of a pair of
twins,' he informed her, and she felt her heart stop beating.

'No!' she moaned in anguish, grabbing for his arm
with hands that trembled uncontrollably. 'I only left them
a few minutes ago. How could this have happened?'

The whole department was run with stringent
security to prevent anything like this happening, every
baby issued with a tracking tag as soon as they were
born so that they couldn't be taken past the sensors
without setting off an alarm.

'I have to go back up,' she declared, and made a
beeline for the lifts.

All the way up to the fourth floor her brain was
whirling with questions. Had anyone contacted Gideon?
Did he know that one of his precious babies had been
stolen?

How had the kidnapper accessed the unit? If he
wasn't the parent of one of their tiny charges he
wouldn't have been given the key code to open the door.

Then the worst question of all formed inside her head. Had Laszlo done this? Had he taken Gideon's child because *she* was the one caring for them? Was this *her* fault because she hadn't left as soon as she'd recognised him?

CHAPTER NINE

NADIA'S hand was shaking so much that she could barely tap out the code on the security pad. And then she was stumbling into the unit, her feet drawn inexorably towards the glass wall of the nursery…to see a scene of utter tranquillity within.

Where were the police? Where were the security guards?

All she could see was Jenny beside the isolette, smiling as she checked one of the monitor leads, her mouth moving as if she was speaking soothing words to the two babies sleeping soundly…

Two babies?

She blinked and looked again, wondering if she was simply seeing what she wanted to see rather than what was actually there.

'Jenny?' She didn't dare do any more than stick her head around the door with a mask held over her face. The last thing she wanted to do was introduce a potentially deadly infectious organism into the nursery. 'Are they all right?'

'Of course they are. Why wouldn't they be?' she

demanded with a slight edge to her voice, as though hurt that Nadia would doubt her care.

'I was stopped by Security. They said someone had kidnapped a baby from the fourth floor…one of twins…and I immediately thought…I was afraid…'

Nadia didn't know how to finish the sentence. She could hardly tell the young woman that she'd been convinced that it was one of Gideon's babies who'd been stolen, and that Laszlo was behind the theft because of *her*.

'Oh, Lord above,' Jenny said in a shocked voice. 'How could anyone even *think* of doing such a thing? And how would they get the baby out of the hospital? Surely the electronic tags are there to prevent that happening.'

Nadia was trembling in the aftermath of the rush of adrenaline and would need to sit down with a strong cup of coffee before she made another attempt to go home.

In the meantime, a glance along the corridor gave her just a fleeting glimpse of one of the security guards with the company insignia emblazoned on each epaulette. The sight jogged something in her memory, but she was too jittery to think what it was. Perhaps, when she'd found that coffee, she'd be able to get her brain working properly again. All she could think of now was that Amy and Adam were safe and well and Gideon wasn't having to face the heartbreak of losing one of those precious babies.

'Gideon!' As if her thoughts had conjured him up, there he was, sprawled out in the most comfortable of the available chairs. 'I thought you'd be on duty by now.'

'I thought you'd be home, putting your feet up with a big cup of tea,' he countered, and made getting out of the sagging cushion look effortless. 'What brings you back? Surely they didn't call you in for a double shift?'

'I never made it home,' she said, grateful to sit down before she fell down. To go through that much stress at the end of a long day on her feet wasn't good, and her feet had been aching before she'd run all the way up the stairs to the fourth floor. 'Security stopped me at the main doors and searched my bag to see if I was the one who'd just kidnapped a baby—one of twins.'

'What!' Shock had him whirling towards her with the kettle in his hand without remembering to turn off the tap, and the water hit the sink full force to shower across his back, soaking the thin cotton of his scrubs and plastering it against his torso.

He gasped and quickly rectified the situation, giving her an enticing view of an unexpectedly muscular torso before he turned back to face her again.

'What baby?' he demanded, already striding towards the door.

'Stop, Gideon!' she called, silently cursing herself for not making it perfectly clear that Amy and Adam weren't involved. 'They're safe. It's *not* one of yours,' she added, and saw the tension leave him like the air leaking from a balloon.

There was a knock at the door and he was still close enough to reach out to open it immediately, startling the officer on the other side for a second.

'I'm sorry to disturb you, Doctor,' he said formally, the ubiquitous notepad in his hand, 'but we're making enquiries in case anyone saw anything suspicious within the last hour. Can you tell me what time you arrived on the fourth floor and if you saw anyone acting in a suspicious manner?'

Nadia had to bite back a chuckle, in spite of the

serious situation. The man sounded so much like the stereotypical stage policeman that it was hard to keep a straight face, especially when she caught an answering glint in Gideon's eyes.

She listened quietly while the officer went through his questions but all the while there was something nagging at the back of her mind…something that she really should be able to recall…something—or someone…

'There was a man!' she exclaimed suddenly, startling them all. 'I'm sorry,' she apologised hastily, 'but I just remembered.'

'Where was this man, miss, and when did you see him?' There was a new intensity to the officer's questions and he made her think of a dog who had just found the scent of something important and had no intention of losing it.

'I don't remember exactly when I saw him for the first time,' she admitted, and the man almost seemed to wilt with the vagueness of her answer. 'He's been here at least three times, and at first I thought he must be the husband of a woman in labour. Someone who had come out of the room to get a breath of air, perhaps?'

'Are you sure that isn't what he was?' the policeman challenged. 'It took nearly thirty hours for my first one to be born.'

'But *you* probably weren't wandering the corridors dressed in an overcoat while she was in labour,' Nadia retorted. 'And *you* weren't wearing a hat with the peak pulled down so that the CCTV cameras wouldn't be able to see your face.'

The more she thought about it, the more shifty the man's behaviour seemed. And even though she was certain that it had been the same man each time she'd seen him, she still couldn't be certain what his face looked like. It could even have been Laszlo…but, no, that didn't feel right. She didn't have the same feeling of menace that she'd felt when she'd been so aware of the sensation of being watched as she'd crossed the hospital grounds.

'Which cameras would have caught him?' The man seemed almost excited now as he pressed the keys on his phone. 'The security team can let us look at the footage if we know where you saw him and a rough time.'

'I can show you,' Nadia offered, her tired feet suddenly forgotten as she leapt to them and led the way out into the unit.

She pointed to the bank of lifts in the wide stretch of corridor that joined the highly specialised prema-ture baby unit with the rest of the obs/gyn and mater-nity departments.

'About half an hour ago, he was standing by the lifts as if he couldn't make up his mind whether to press the button.' She paused a moment to get the sequence of events in her head and to censor the part where she'd con-vinced herself that Laszlo had discovered where she worked. 'I overbalanced and he grabbed my arm to steady me, but then he set off along the corridor in that direction.' She pointed away from the unit they'd just left.

'Exactly what was he wearing?' The man's pen was flying across the page as he took every detail down.

'A hat with a peak and a rather shabby, rather large overcoat that didn't look as if it belonged to him, unless he'd lost a lot of weight. Except…'

She frowned, because in her final image of him, just

before he'd entered the toilets at the end of the corridor, the coat had seemed to fit him better, as though he'd suddenly put the weight back on.

'He went into the toilets,' she gasped and set off at a run. 'The man went into the visitors' toilets and I think he had something hidden under his coat.'

She might have started running first, but the two men had longer legs and both had overtaken her by the time they reached the cloakroom door. Gideon's hand hit the door first but the officer was first into the room beyond.

The room was empty.

There were no red-faced men at the short row of urinals and there were only two cubicles with doors and neither lock was engaged.

Except she didn't think they were both empty, in spite of appearances.

For the first time in her life she voluntarily entered this all-male domain, approaching the almost closed door of the second cubicle on silent feet. A passing glimpse of herself in the mirrors over the basins told her that she looked completely ridiculous, like a cartoon cat creeping up on an unsuspecting mouse, but then she heard a rustling noise that certainly shouldn't be coming from the cubicle if it really was empty.

A hand fastened around her arm and she nearly squeaked until she saw that it was Gideon, holding her back and gesturing for her to let the officer lead the way.

Nadia was frustrated that she wasn't the one to push the door open. From the position by the door that Gideon had drawn her back to, she didn't even have a view of the interior of the cubicle, until she realised that the mirrors reflected them perfectly.

That was why she was able to see that, when the policeman gently swung the door open, he revealed the man she'd seen, but this time he was sitting on the lid of the toilet with the missing baby on his lap while he frantically sawed away at the security tag with a metal file.

There were tears streaming down his cheeks and his expression looked no more dangerous than that of a rabbit caught in the headlights of a car when the officer said, 'I think you'd better come with me, sir.'

'D-don't take him away,' the man stammered, abandoning his fruitless attempt to remove the security tag. 'Th-they've got another one. Th-they don't need him, n-not like Sally and m-me. W-we need him. We'd l-love him…s-so much.'

Nadia almost felt sorry for the man as she carried the infant out to find the nearest paediatrician for a quick check-up before he was returned to his frantic mother. She could only imagine what circumstances had driven him to do something so desperate. She knew only too well how the traumatic loss of a child had changed her life for ever.

It was another hour before she was ready to leave the hospital, an hour in which she'd sat and talked idly with Gideon while they'd waited for confirmation that the baby had been returned safe and sound to his mother.

They'd also learned that the man and his wife had exhausted their savings and put themselves in serious debt in their failed attempts at IVF. Their last attempt had resulted in a spontaneous abortion at four months, in spite of the consultant's best efforts and far too soon for Nadia's unit to have been able to do anything to help, and had coincided with hearing that one of their fellow IVF patients had just delivered twins.

'That must have been the last straw,' Gideon had said thoughtfully, 'the reason why he flipped.' And she somehow knew that he was thinking about his ex-wife and the way she'd become completely obsessed with the idea of carrying her own child.

'Basic biology,' Nadia whispered, feeling the empty ache inside her and wondering if it would ever go away. 'The fundamental animal need to procreate, to leave some part of your genetic inheritance behind when you leave the world.'

She'd felt that overwhelming need once, so she could understand it.

In spite of the way in which her baby had come into being, once she'd known Anya was inside her she had loved her, bonding with the fact that half of every cell contained *her* DNA that was multiplying and growing with every day, until…until Laszlo had found out she was pregnant.

'Are you ready to go home?' Gideon's prosaic question snapped her out of the nightmare that had been about to overtake her. She was about to be her usual evasive self when he continued, 'I walked in to spend time with Adam and Amy, so I'll be walking back and stopping off to get some food on the way. I live in one of the flats in the road that goes past the cinema. Which way do you go?'

She was surprised to discover just how close they had been living all this time. 'I'm going in the same general direction, but I live on the other side of the main road, in one of the streets behind the railway station.'

She didn't need his swiftly controlled grimace to tell her that it wasn't the nicest area. In fact, the building she lived in had once been an old workhouse, converted into accommodation in a rather rough-and-ready way, but the rent was affordable and it was close enough to walk backwards and forwards to the hospital so that she didn't need the expense of a car or public transport.

'Will you join me for a meal?' he asked, the words sounding very casual, but she knew him well enough to know that her answer mattered to him somehow. Did he feel like celebrating the fact that the missing baby had been recovered uninjured, or did he just not want to eat alone?

Whatever the answer, she'd been so relieved that the whole kidnapping business had not had anything to do with Laszlo after all, that she felt like accepting a man's invitation for the first time since the age of sixteen.

'As long as it isn't anywhere expensive,' she warned, trying to tamp down the sudden feeling of giddy excitement. 'I'll be paying for my own meal and we don't all earn doctor's salaries, you know.'

'In that case, we can go to the little place just round the corner from my flat. The prices are reasonable and the service is friendly…and there's no washing-up to do at the end of the meal.'

'Always a bonus at the end of a busy day,' she agreed on a chuckle, wondering if this was how other women felt when they set out to spend an evening with a man they admired and respected.

Except, if she was honest with herself, what she felt for Gideon was far more than admiration and respect.

Even while she'd been shoring up the walls of her decision to keep a safe distance between the two of them—something that she'd had no trouble doing with any other man—he'd somehow found his own way around the previously insurmountable obstacle to find a place in her heart.

The realisation that she loved him was bitter-sweet.

She'd honestly believed that she would never be able to get past the horrors she'd endured, and the realisation that she had met a man so honest and trustworthy that she'd actually been able to let down her guard was only balanced by the recognition that there could never be a future for her with him. In all honesty, she couldn't contemplate having a relationship with a man without warning him about the effects her past might have on their future together, and she'd tried too hard to leave those memories behind to ever want to tell anyone about them.

Still, that didn't mean that she couldn't enjoy the friendship that he seemed to be offering as they found topic after topic to discuss over their delicious meal.

'That's where I live,' he said, pointing to a beautifully restored Victorian house as they strolled almost aimlessly away from the restaurant.

'Nice,' she said, hoping she didn't sound envious. It was a far cry from hers, even though the two buildings dated from the same era and stood little more than a quarter of a mile apart. It was far nicer than anything she was ever going to be able to afford on a nurse's salary, even a nurse as highly qualified as she was. That didn't mean that she didn't love her job. She did, passionately, believing that in some small way she was atoning for Anya's death with each frail baby she nursed.

'Nadia?' The tone of his voice told her that it wasn't the first time he'd tried to attract her attention and she silently cursed the fact that she seemed unable to stop herself disappearing into the labyrinths of her memories these days.

'I'm sorry. I must be more tired than I thought,' she apologised quickly. 'Thank you for being such good company this evening. Perhaps I'll see you tomorrow?' And before he could offer to escort her to her door she hurriedly crossed the road and set off in the direction of her bed sit.

She'd only been back a few minutes when there was an unexpected knock at her door.

'Gideon?' she breathed, wondering if he'd decided to follow her home to make certain that she was safe. She didn't know whether to be flattered that he would care enough to do such a thing or cross that he now knew where she lived. She'd been at great pains not to let any of her hospital colleagues know her address so that none of them would be able to inadvertently give it to anyone who might be looking for her.

The knock came again, louder this time, and she realised that Gideon might be standing out there, worrying that something had happened to her.

She was just reaching for the first of the locks to release it when the knocking became an angry banging and she heard the sound of her worst nightmares.

'Open the door, bitch!' snarled Laszlo in the tone she'd hoped she would never have to hear again.

Just the sound of it was enough to make her cower back against the wall as he spewed a stream of foul invective.

'You owe me!' he shouted, switching to English, and she cringed at the knowledge that everyone in the house would be able to hear him. 'I gave your father good money and you've barely started to repay me.'

The door was shuddering under his repeated blows and she began to wonder if the locks she'd installed as soon as she'd moved in would be able to withstand his anger. There were three of them, as well as a bolt at the top and the bottom of the door, but she still wasn't certain that it would be enough when he was in this sort of temper.

She hadn't heard more than a passing snatch of her own language in years but she had no trouble understanding him when he switched back to his native tongue.

'You'd better come out of your own accord, and fast, or I'll call for Mihal,' he warned with a sadistic chuckle that turned her blood cold. 'He knows how to make you sorry. Remember?'

She shuddered and barely stifled a whimper. Oh, yes, she remembered only too well what Mihal would do to her to make her sorry, and for one dreadful moment almost gave in to Laszlo's demands, just so that the hulking brute wouldn't be given permission to do it all over again.

A muted bleeping told her that she was too late, that Laszlo was already using a mobile phone to call Mihal to deal with her door. It was only his expression of disgust that reminded her that it was almost impossible to get a decent signal anywhere in that corridor that made her think she had any chance of escaping him.

Thanking God for the fact that she'd had the forethought to be prepared, she hurried to the other side of her bed and retrieved the precious store of money from under the loose floorboard, grabbed the small bag from where she'd left it ready in the cupboard, stuffed with the few things she couldn't bear to leave behind, and snatched her handbag off the little hall table beside her front door even as she was reaching to release the first lock.

Her hands were shaking so badly by the time she got to the third one that it took her two attempts to open it, all the while desperately aware of the seconds flying past. By now Laszlo would have reached the front door of the building and discovered that the signal was finally strong enough to make his call. Then he would return to wait for Mihal to join him at her door, making sure to tell her in excruciating detail what was going to happen to her when he got his hands on her again.

'Well, this time it *isn't* going to happen, not if I can help it,' she muttered as she sped lightly up the nearby stairs to knock on the door of the only other young woman living in the house, her other hand pressing on the button of the doorbell for good measure.

'Maria?' she called hoarsely, when everything inside her wanted to scream for help as loudly as she could, then she had the sudden terrifying thought that her neighbour might not be home. In that case, she would be caught up here like a rat in a trap without even a door between her and Laszlo's idea of vengeance.

'Nadia? Is that you?' said a sleepy-sounding voice on the other side of the door.

'Yes!' She swallowed convulsively when she heard the ominous sound of male footsteps downstairs, walking swiftly along the corridor directly below her towards her room. 'Can…can I come in for a minute? Please?'

Her neighbour's hesitation was understandable. The two of them had done little more than exchange bland pleasantries when they'd passed in the entrance hall, both of them apparently equally averse to forming close friendships with chance neighbours.

She could have wept with relief when she heard the unmistakable sound of a bolt being drawn back and almost tripped over Maria's feet in her urgency to get behind the safety of a closed door.

'Nadia!' Maria exclaimed, clearly startled by her precipitate entry, 'What on earth…?' Then something in her face must have told her young neighbour that this was something more serious than an inept attempt at a social visit. 'What is it? What's happened?' she demanded, her dark eyes sharp with a knowledge of things that a girl her age shouldn't have to know. 'Man trouble?'

Nadia nodded. 'Bad,' she said succinctly, grateful that Maria didn't seem to need any more words to explain the situation.

'What do you need?' the young woman asked briskly. 'Shall I phone the police for you?'

Nadia shook her head frantically. She had survived this long by lying low, and what could she prove? Nothing more than a man knocking on her door. Besides that, Laszlo had the connections to allow him to disappear at will, only to return when the coast was clear to take up where he'd left off.

'Wait till I've gone,' she pleaded. 'I don't want to get stuck here, answering questions.'

'I'll tell them I heard a lot of shouting and screaming. Will that do?'

'Thanks. It might slow him down.' She nearly managed a smile, but her heart was beating so fast that it was almost impossible to think straight.

'Could I borrow your mobile phone?' she asked, suddenly realising that there was only one person in the whole world that she could go to for help…only one person she *wanted* to go to.

'Of course you can.' She held it out straight away. 'Then you can use my window to get to the fire escape.'

Nadia nodded her agreement, but she was already concentrating on dialling the number she'd used every time she'd needed to report yet another setback in either Amy's or Adam's progress.

'Gideon?' she said when he answered after just three rings, her voice vibrating with the terror filling her veins. 'Please…I need your help'

Gideon was pacing backwards and forwards in front of the window, half-convinced that he must have dreamed that frantic phone call.

Nadia was usually the epitome of calm and serenity so it was hardly surprising that he hadn't recognised her voice for a moment. Then he'd realised that she was in some sort of trouble and every protective instinct he possessed had leapt to attention.

He'd immediately suggested that he should drive round to her flat to collect her but Nadia had begged him to stay where he was.

'It will be easier if I come to you,' she'd said, and even over the poor reception of the call he was sure he could hear her teeth chattering.

'What on earth's going on?' he demanded of the darkened room, his eyes fixed on the road he'd seen her crossing such a short time ago, peering through the driving rain that had suddenly started to fall. 'If anyone's hurt her…' His hands clenched into fists as visions of vengeance filled his mind.

He already knew that she'd suffered some sort of trauma in her past, otherwise she wouldn't have been so jumpy every time he'd gone near her. It had taken patience he'd never known he possessed to give her the time to recognise that he was a person she could trust.

But the last thing he would have wanted was to find out that she trusted him because something bad had happened to her.

'Where is she?' he demanded when there was no sign of her familiar slender body hurrying towards him along the road. Was she one of the people huddled under umbrellas who were scurrying to reach their destinations?

Then there was a knock at his door and he had to stifle a curse. Which one of his fellow residents was visiting him *now*? He needed to keep his vigil for Nadia, needed to stay close to the security phone linked to the front door of the building so that he could buzz her in as quickly as possible. If she'd been hurt and needed to be taken to A and E…

'Yes?' he said curtly as he dragged the door open with one eye towards the front window, hoping his tone was sufficiently offputting to dissuade whichever neighbour it was from wanting to keep him talking.

'Gideon?'

He nearly gave himself whiplash his head turned towards her exotic voice so quickly. How on earth had she managed to get into the building without ringing the bell? For that matter, how had she managed to approach the building without him catching so much as a glimpse of her?

Not that he would have recognised her looking like this, he admitted as he stood back to let her enter. She looked as if she was soaked to the skin, wearing nothing more than when he'd seen her earlier. The only thing different was the small backpack hooked over her shoulders that thudded against the door when she slumped back against it, gasping for breath.

Her eyes were wild, darting here and there, and she was trembling all over. He was reminded of a kitten he'd once rescued from a pursuing dog.

'What on earth happened?' he demanded, wishing he had the right to wrap her in his arms. He could almost hear her bones rattling as she shook. 'Were you attacked? Are you hurt?'

'No…I'm not hurt,' she managed to gasp. 'I got away, but only through Maria's window.'

Suddenly, the enormity of what she'd just gone through seemed to dawn on her and without a second's warning she started to crumple to the floor.

'Whoa!' he exclaimed and swooped her up into his arms. There hadn't been time to wonder about her reaction to the contact or she could have ended up with some spectacular bruises. As it was, instead of trying to preserve her usual distance between them, she actually flung an arm around his neck and burrowed her face into his shoulder.

'I thought I was trapped…thought I'd never get away,' she muttered through chattering teeth. 'Then his phone wouldn't work… He had to go to the front door…I grabbed my bag…my money… Ran upstairs…'

'Shh…shh,' he soothed, not really caring what she was trying to tell him in those disjointed, heavily accented snatches. The most important thing, as far as he was concerned, was that she was finally in his arms and letting him take care of her for a change, and he couldn't have cared less that she'd instantly soaked him to the skin on contact. 'There's plenty of time to tell me all about it later,' he suggested, and was taken aback when Nadia shook her head violently.

'No, no!' she said, pushing against his chest so that she could lean far enough back to be able to see his face. 'Gideon, it is danger, still. Maria phones the police, but they can do nothing if they do not know about the girls. And if they take Laszlo away, who will feed them? Who will protect them from the others?'

'Laszlo?' Jealous rage roared through him at the sound of a man's name, even though it was obvious that she had absolutely no tender feelings for whoever he was. 'Nadia, who is Laszlo?'

'He is a bad man…an evil man,' she insisted, and the fear he saw in her eyes was dreadful. 'Maria is phoning police but they will talk and because there is no one to tell them the truth…no one who will dare to stand against him…he will be free in the morning and he will search and search until…until…'

She was already shaking as a result of the icy rain and when she started to sob, too, harsh, raw sounds that seemed as if they would wrench her slender body in two, he had to sit down with her or risk dropping her.

'Nadia, sweetheart…' She seemed as oblivious to the endearment that slipped out as she was to the fact that he was now cradling her on his lap with both arms wrapped around her. She really needed to strip off her soaked clothing and get into something dry, but he didn't think she was ready for something that would make her feel that vulnerable.

'Please, Nadia…I don't understand.' There was something about her agitation that told him it would be wrong to wait until she'd calmed down. Whatever situation she'd just fled from was serious enough that something needed to be done as quickly as possible. 'Who is Laszlo? Why were you running away from him? Is he a violent man… dangerous? Do you need me to call the police?'

'Ah, Gideon, the police will be able to do nothing,' she said with despair in her eyes. 'He is too clever. I can prove nothing against him and he will make me pay for reporting him…' He wasn't sure whether she was sobbing again or if that was the start of hysterical laughter.

'Nadia, we have good police officers assigned to the A and E department. I know them well because I see so much of them,' he explained, absolutely certain that they would be able to help her if only she would trust him enough to tell him what was going on. 'Tell me who this man is and what he's done to you and we'll make certain he can't hurt you again.'

The expression on her face was one he'd never seen before and the utter hopelessness of it broke his heart.

'You can't,' she whispered sadly. 'Nothing can stop Laszlo. He is too powerful…too rich…too…' She shook her head.

'But *who* is he? How do you know him? Is he from your own country?'

It felt cruel to badger her for answers when she was in such a fragile state, but if he was going to have a chance to protect her, he needed the information that only she could give.

'Yes, he is from my country,' she said in a strangely dead voice. 'He made an arrangement with my father so my brother can have the money to go to university, but I did not know this. I thought…' She drew in a shuddering breath and gave a sharp bark of self-deprecating laughter. 'I thought I was going to be his wife…I saw the papers and there was a ceremony, but it was all a…a pretend…a lie. As soon as we go to his place there were men waiting because he had told them he was going to fetch a new girl…a virgin…and they would pay good money—bid against each other to be the first to—'

'Shh, shh,' he soothed, his mind churning with the horrific pictures she'd painted. He rocked her as if she were a little child as she cried in his arms and he didn't know when he'd ever felt more helpless or more blindingly angry.

CHAPTER TEN

'NADIA?'

The voice was soft and concerned and unmistakably Gideon's but it still took her several seconds to drag her gaze up to meet those beautiful green eyes.

It had been past midnight by the time the police inspector had left the flat and she was still sitting huddled in the corner of his settee with a thick quilt wrapped around her shoulders, feeling as lifeless as a puppet with the strings cut.

'You must be exhausted,' he said, and she supposed he must be right, but she knew she wouldn't be getting sleep any time soon. Her nerves were so jangled that it felt as if she might fly apart into a million pieces at the slightest thing.

'Come on.' He held one lean hand out in invitation. 'It's time you got some rest.'

She stared at his hand for several seconds, unable to work out what he wanted her to do with it, then he made a little beckoning gesture and it dawned on her.

'I should go back to my own—' she began, then stopped with a grimace, remembering the policeman's description of the destruction that Mihal had wreaked at Laszlo's behest. There was no way she could go back there tonight. In fact, she would probably never be able to go back there, ever, with the memories of what had so nearly happened there.

'There's a bed waiting for you and I've just made it up with clean bedding, so don't let my efforts go to waste,' he added with a hint of a twinkle that convinced her that it would be safe to put her hand in his. She certainly didn't have the strength to get off the settee under her own steam, not with her legs still trembling the way they were. She didn't think she'd ever run so fast in all her life, not even the first time she'd escaped from Laszlo. Added to that, she'd had to take such a round-about route so as not to lead anyone to Gideon's door that it had more then doubled the distance.

'Here you are,' he said as he paused in the doorway and gestured inside the room. 'You know where the en suite is. If there's anything else you need…?'

'But this is *your* room,' she objected, feeling more miserable than ever at the situation. Everything was so different from earlier that evening. Then, she had actually been foolish enough to think that there might be a chance of something…something *more* between the two of them. She should have known that once any decent man heard what she'd done…what she'd been…a huge gulf would be bound to open up between the two of them.

It had been bad enough having to tell him the bare bones of her story, but the way it had flooded out of her like that, she really hadn't been able to stop it. But then to know that Gideon was sitting there, listening, while she'd spelt it out to the policeman in all its nightmarish details, had been almost more than she could bear.

She hadn't even been able to force herself to look across at him, knowing that the protective wall that he'd been persistently demolishing week by week as she'd cared for his babies was going to have to be built up again, brick by painful brick, until she could hide behind her protective shield again.

'Will you be all right?' he asked softly, and for just a moment it looked as if he might reach out to stroke her face, but then his hand dropped to his side and she knew that there would be no more touching. Why would he want to touch someone who'd been—?

'You can leave the light on if you want to,' he suggested, breaking into her dark thoughts. 'And if there's anything else you need, all you've got to do is call. I'll be close by, so I'll hear if you…'

The shadows in those deep green eyes and the hint of a frown pleating his forehead under the unruly strands of dark hair were silent evidence that, in spite of everything he had heard this evening, he was still the same caring, kind man that he'd always been.

Without a second's warning the floodgates finally burst.

'Oh, Gideon…' she wailed as the tears began to stream down her cheeks, and to her utter relief he didn't hesitate for a second before he swept her up into his arms.

Those arms were so strong and made her feel so secure as he cradled her on his lap, settling himself against his headboard while her body tried to cleanse itself of so many years of misery and fear.

It wasn't until the flood had finally dwindled to a trickle that she realised that he'd tucked her head in the curve of his shoulder that seemed to have been made just for her, and there, now that her sobs had quietened to intermittent hiccups, she discovered that she could hear his heartbeat, steady, strong, reassuring...all the things that were the essence of Gideon himself.

She was so exhausted that she couldn't resist staying just where she was for a little while longer, enjoying the simplicity of listening to the steady rhythms of life while, for the first time she could remember, she soaked up the delight of being held as if she mattered...as if someone actually cared about her.

Even as sleep started to overtake her she knew that thought was just an illusion, especially now that Gideon knew all her ugly secrets. He was taking care of her for tonight because she didn't have anywhere else to go, but after that he probably wouldn't want to have anything more to do with her. That thought hurt far worse than anything Laszlo had done to her, as did the realisation that Gideon probably wouldn't want someone like her taking care of his precious babies either.

Gideon knew exactly when Nadia fell asleep in his arms but he had no intention of letting her go, even to tuck her under the covers in his bed.

He was still slightly in shock with everything that had happened in the last few hours, but in case this was the only time that he was ever granted the opportunity to hold her, he had no intention of wasting a single second.

He'd known almost from the first day he'd met her that she was someone special, but he'd never realised just how extraordinary until he'd listened to the awful details she'd related to the officers tonight.

He could no more understand the actions of a father who would sacrifice his daughter to provide for his son than he could condone a man like Laszlo growing rich from the misery of innocent young girls.

But the one thought that repeated itself over and over in his head as he cradled this indomitable woman in his arms was how much he respected her and how proud he was of everything she'd achieved after such a destructive start to her life.

He'd been attracted to her... Hah! What was he thinking? He'd been falling in love with her almost from the first time he'd seen how tenderly she'd cared for his fragile babies. And that was in spite of the fact that Norah's abandonment had made him wary of opening himself up to any sort of new relationship.

Nadia had been reserved, too, but it was no wonder that she'd been so wary of allowing anything other than a strictly work-related connection between them. He wouldn't really be surprised if she'd never been able to allow another man to touch her, and the fact that she'd actually let him cradle her on his lap while she cried those long-overdue tears gave him hope.

Unfortunately, he'd also seen the way she'd withdrawn inside herself with every word she'd spoken to the police and, in spite of the fact that her information was even now assisting in the breaking of one of the vice rings that had been plaguing the country for far too long, he'd recognised the signs that told him she was rebuilding the wall between herself and the rest of the world.

It was frustrating, especially when this evening he'd actually felt as if he was managing to put a few cracks in that wall. He'd even begun to hope that it wouldn't be too long before he could persuade her that she couldn't bear to lose contact with Adam and Amy. He

certainly wasn't too proud to use her obvious attachment
to the twins for his own ends, because if she wanted to
continue seeing them, that meant he wouldn't be losing
contact with her either.

And one day…maybe…she might learn to trust him
enough to become a permanent part of their lives…
perhaps some time before those two precious babies
were old enough to have babies of their own? he added
glumly.

He stifled a wry chuckle at that thought, knowing he
would go screaming around the bend long before that
if he couldn't find some way to hold her in his arms on
a regular basis.

He didn't know when it had happened, but having
Nadia in his life seemed to have become as essential to
him as breathing, and that meant that he had some
serious thinking to do if he was going to find a way to
persuade her to take a chance on him.

'Gideon?' she murmured drowsily, and he nearly
groaned aloud when she nuzzled against his throat like
a sleepy kitten.

Suddenly he felt her grow rigid in his arms and he knew
that she'd either remembered tonight's events or she'd
realised that she was far too close to him for comfort.

'It's all right, Nadia,' he soothed, reluctantly loosen-
ing his hold on her so that she could put as much
distance between them as she needed. 'Tuck yourself
into bed and I'll leave you in peace.'

'No,' she whimpered, clutching his shirt and pressing
herself against him as if he was her only shelter. 'Don't
go. I don't want to be alone.'

'If you're certain?' He tightened his hold on her

again, marvelling at how perfectly she seemed to belong there with him.

It felt wrong to be grateful that she was too scared for him to leave her, but at the moment he'd take any concession he could get. When he'd heard the fear in her voice, he'd been terrified that phone call would be the last time he ever heard from her. To be given permission to hold her close like this was far more than he'd expected.

'I'm certain,' she whispered against his throat and the soft puffs of air sent shivers up and down his spine.

He felt her relax against him and thought she was falling asleep again until she began to speak, her voice as insubstantial as mist in the dimly lit room.

'I've been lonely for so many years,' she confessed, almost as if she was admitting to a weakness. He wanted to reassure her that none of it had been her fault but knew it was more important to let her take things at her own pace.

'I couldn't let anyone get too close because I couldn't tell anyone who I really was,' she continued. 'I didn't dare, because I was certain that Laszlo was still looking for me... He would never give up while he believed I still owed him for the money he gave my f-father.'

She drew in a jagged breath and he knew that was one betrayal he would probably never be able to forgive the man who should have protected her.

'And also because I couldn't trust anyone enough to let them come near me...couldn't be sure that they wouldn't hurt me, too.'

'You can trust me,' he said through the ache in his throat that grew with every minute that he fought tears of his own.

Suddenly he had a flash of memory of that young girl

who'd been brought into A and E not long ago. She'd been the same age as Nadia when she'd first been brutalised, not much more than a child.

'I know I can trust you…I trusted you with my life when I phoned you,' she said with a new strength to her voice that gave him hope.

Did he dare push her now? Was it too soon after recent events or was it best to give her the certainty of knowing that he wanted something long term with her?

'Could you do it again?' he asked, hoping she couldn't hear the way his pulse had started to gallop, but there was nothing he could do about it. This woman meant as much to him as those fragile babies she'd been caring for, and his life would be utterly empty without them.

'Could I do what?' Was that wariness he heard in her voice or was she too exhausted for such a conversation at this time of night? He hoped not, because the words he needed to say were burning a hole in his tongue.

'Could you trust me with your life? Could you trust me to make you happy?' Words could never encompass everything he wanted to say, but he had no other way of asking.

He was certain he'd made a mess of everything when she didn't speak for a long time, certain that she was trying to find the kindest way to tell him that there was no hope that she could ever—

'What do you mean, Gideon? What are you asking for?'

He had to swallow the lump of fear in his throat before he could answer. 'I'm asking for you to trust me enough to marry me.'

'No!' The refusal was instant and he didn't need the

fierce shake of her head to reinforce her refusal. The roaring sound in his ears almost drowned out the fact that she was speaking again.

'Gideon, it's not possible. You *can't* want to marry me, not when you know all those things about me, not when I might never be able to…to be a normal wife to you. You need someone who—'

'*You*, Nadia. I need *you*,' he interrupted, put gentle fingertips to her mouth to silence her argument, then continued, 'I want to marry you and live with you for the rest of our lives and I would *still* want to marry you even if I knew I was never going to be able to do anything more than hold you in my arms each night.'

'But…' The expression in her eyes was a mixture of bewilderment and hope.

'Believe in me, Nadia. Believe in my love,' he said persuasively, his heart in his mouth. 'Say yes.'

'Oh, help! I think I'm going to be sick again,' Dani muttered in an aside to Nadia as they waited for the music to begin.

'Try taking a deep breath and concentrate on blowing it out slowly,' Nadia murmured. It was one of the few tricks she knew, dating from the time when she'd finally realised what was wrong with her all those years ago. 'And think good thoughts,' she added. 'You don't want Josh to see you looking green when you join him at the altar.'

'It's *his* fault I'm feeling sick,' Dani grumbled. 'If he hadn't been so stubborn, I wouldn't have had to seduce him and we'd have remembered to take precautions.'

'I think that comes under the heading of too much information.' Nadia chuckled, hoping that it was jealousy tying her nerves in knots rather than terror at the thought of the coming night.

With a baby already on the way, it was obvious that Dani and Josh had anticipated their wedding vows, while she and Gideon…

She threw a glance in his direction, able to see him standing beside Josh from her position by the door, and her heart did that same crazy dance as it had just an hour ago in the registry office when the two of them had stood in front of the registrar to make their own vows.

Gideon had tried to persuade her to make it a double wedding with Dani and Josh, sharing the same venue for the ceremony as well as the reception, but she couldn't. Somehow, the memories of everything she'd gone through—everything she'd been forced to do—and especially the fact that she'd been unable to stop them killing Anya before she'd had a chance to draw a single breath…all of that had left her with a sense of guilt that, even though her logical mind knew it was unwarranted, her heart wouldn't let her stand in a church to make her vows.

And Gideon had understood.

Irrational though it may have seemed to anyone who hadn't lived through it, the moment she'd tried to put the words together to explain her feelings, he'd immediately agreed that the actual venue for their wedding didn't matter to him so much as the fact that they would be making their promises to each other.

At the altar Dani turned to hand her bouquet to Nadia, the expression of joy on her face showing that all thoughts of morning sickness had been banished. Gideon's strong arm wrapped around Nadia's shoul-

ders and guided her to their designated pew, and a brief
glance at their assembled friends, relatives and colleagues showed more than one eye bright with the hint
of joyful tears.

The brief sadness that there hadn't been any
members of her own family to share her unexpected
happiness was dispelled when Gideon murmured, 'Is
everything all right?'

'Perfect,' she whispered back, and hoped that he
couldn't see the growing nervousness behind her smile.
Amy and Adam were probably going to be ready for
release by the end of the week and, after the wedding
reception, there was also all the new nursery furniture
to assemble in readiness for their arrival.

And none of that was the reason for the panicky
jitters that were tightening the coil of anxiety inside her
until she didn't know whether to wish that the day would
go on for ever or to want it to be over and done with.

'Relax,' Gideon soothed, his words for her ears alone
under the bright chatter and laughter of the people surrounding them.

All day he'd been aware that Nadia was wound tighter
than a violin string, and at first had thought it was because
she was thinking about backing out of the marriage.

Not that he would have let her, because her belief
that he could find someone far better to marry was
nonsense. Then he'd wondered whether she was
nervous about appearing in front of their friends and
colleagues for the first time without the disguise she'd
adopted to hide her identity.

'It might take me a little time to get used to the real

you, but you look beautiful,' he teased, taking in the soft sunshine blonde of the hair that had been hidden under the nondescript brown dye and the striking turquoise eyes that had been revealed when she'd removed the coloured contact lenses. 'Not that I didn't like the way you looked before,' he added quickly, and pressed a kiss to the silky skin at her temple.

If anything, his reassurance only seemed to make her grow more tense and he began to wonder if she was already regretting their vows. Or perhaps it was nothing more than a habit for her, after living with terror for so many years?

'Laszlo's behind bars,' he reminded her, the news passed on by the policeman who'd questioned Nadia the night she'd run to Gideon for protection. 'He won't be able to come after you again.'

Her smile looked more genuine that time, and was filled with satisfaction. The information she'd been able to give the police had enabled them to fit the final pieces to the jigsaw they'd been assembling to give them the full picture of Laszlo's drugs and prostitution empire. As a result, there were now thirty-seven young girls receiving help after they'd been rescued from the brutal life into which he'd forced them, and with the freezing of his bank accounts full of the proceeds of trafficking, it shouldn't be long before it would be as if his evil had never existed…except in the memories of his victims.

But none of that explained the growing look of misery he could see in her eyes. All around them people were having fun celebrating the two weddings, and Josh and Dani were enjoying every moment now that the nausea seemed to have subsided for the day, while he and Nadia…

Finally he couldn't stand it any more.

'Let's say our farewells,' he suggested, knowing that nothing was going to be solved until they had a heart-to-heart conversation, and that certainly wasn't possible in the middle of a crowd of people bent on merrymaking. 'We need to go home.'

'Oh, but—' she began, but something in his expression silenced whatever objection she was going to make. She sighed and her shoulders drooped, and it was the air of resignation about her that squeezed his heart in a vice.

It took nearly an hour to extricate themselves from the cheerful good wishes and teasing advice of their friends and colleagues, and by the time they finally drove away, Gideon was nearly as tense as Nadia.

Their journey to his flat was completely silent and seemed to take for ever, but he spent the time bolstering his determination to solve whatever problem was making his new wife so miserable. It didn't matter what it was, they would deal with it together and get beyond it because now that he was married to the woman he loved, nothing was going to stop him proving that he was committed to taking care of her, heart and soul, for the rest of their lives.

'Would you like a cup of tea…or something to eat?' Nadia offered as soon as he closed the door, already hurrying towards the kitchen as if she couldn't bear to be alone with him for a second.

'I'll make the tea,' he said, catching her elbow and finding that it was almost vibrating with tension. He released it and thrust his hand in his pocket when all he wanted to do was pull her into his arms and reassure her that everything would be all right.

'It's been a long, stressful day…a long stressful couple of months, if we're honest,' he continued, trying hard to sound at ease and knowing that he was failing miserably. 'Why don't you take your time in the bath while I get the tea? Then we can relax and unwind…and talk.'

Nadia took off down the hall like a rabbit with a fox on her tail, leaving him with an ache that didn't feel as if it was going to diminish any time soon.

He took himself off to the shower room he'd added when he'd first bought the flat, needing a few minutes of thinking time before he'd be ready to face her again.

Had he rushed her into marriage because he'd realised that it was what *he* wanted? He'd been so sure after Norah had demanded a divorce that he would never want to put himself through it again, but there had just been something about Nadia…something that had made him absolutely certain that he would never truly be happy without her as his wife and the mother of his children. And he'd been every bit as certain that she would have no difficulty loving Adam and Amy as if they were her own, if she didn't already.

But had she been ready for marriage?

The trauma she'd been through would have destroyed most women, but she hadn't just survived, she'd triumphed by making a new life for herself that was a success by anyone's measure.

Should he offer to have the marriage annulled? To set her free? Would that make her happy…or at least happier than she'd seemed ever since they'd signed their names to the marriage certificate?

His hands were shaking as he arranged cheese and biscuits on the tray with the pot of tea. Neither of them had eaten much at the reception, but the fact that it had been a buffet had probably hidden that fact from their guests. Not that he'd be able to swallow a mouthful now, not with such uncertainty tightening its grip on his throat, but if he could persuade Nadia to have something, perhaps she would start to relax.

He tapped briefly and pushed the door open, then wondered if he should have waited outside when she whirled to face him, wide-eyed. Then he caught sight of the soft silky fabric she was wearing and it was his turn to go wide-eyed. It was certainly a far cry from the over-sized T-shirts he'd retrieved for her from the flat she'd never wanted to visit again.

'Dani gave it to me,' she said in a strangely breathless voice, apparently completely unaware that the light from the en suite behind her gave him a perfect view of her surprisingly long legs and the sweet curves of her hips and waist.

'It's a pretty colour…almost the same as your eyes,' he said when he managed to get his tongue under control and drag his eyes back up to her face.

'It's the most beautiful thing I've ever worn,' she confessed shyly, running her fingertips over the tantalising lace detail around the neckline. 'I never had anything with lace on it before.'

To his surprise, Gideon felt a sudden urge to cry for the little girl…for the *woman*…who'd had to wait until she was twenty-seven to wear a pretty nightdress, and he made a silent promise that Amy wouldn't have to wait nearly that long.

'You don't need lace to make you look beautiful,' he said, the words emerging almost of their own volition, and he was touched to see a wash of soft pink heighten the natural colour of her cheeks.

The cups rattled, drawing his attention away from her embarrassment to the fact that he still had the tray clutched between his white-knuckled hands.

'I made tea,' he said as he deposited it on the bedside cabinet and sat on the edge of the bed. 'And cheese and biscuits.' He glanced over at her, still hovering uncertainly in the doorway, and patted the bed beside him, hoping the gesture looked more casual than it felt. 'Come and join me.'

She perched tentatively on the edge of the bed and only began to relax when he offered her a choice of Brie or Cheddar and made her laugh with a complaint that their colleagues had virtually inhaled the beautiful food at the reception before either of them had tasted a thing.

For several minutes it looked as if he'd managed to allay whatever fears had made her so tense, but one look at the tight grip she was exerting on her cup told him it was just an illusion.

His heart felt like lead in his chest and he was trying to find the words to ask her if she regretted their marriage when she spoke.

'Gideon?' There was an obvious quiver to her voice. 'Please, I want to know…I *need* to know… Is it different?'

He blinked, his brain scrambling to work out what she was talking about. Had he missed something?

'Is *what* different?'

She swallowed, staring down into the empty cup that now had both hands wrapped tightly around it. 'S-sex,' she whispered with a darkening blush, unable to meet his gaze. 'Is sex different when…w-when it's not being paid for? When it's between two people who…who…?'

He desperately wanted to pull her into his arms, but he was afraid she was far too tense to accept that much intimacy so he had to compromise by resting one hand around her bone-white knuckles.

'When it's between two people who love each other it's not called sex, it's called love-making,' he said softly, ducking his head so that he could look up into her down-turned face. 'And, Nadia, while I have no experience of what sex is like with…with a stranger…' at least his brain was working swiftly enough to avoid using the word 'prostitute' '…I can guarantee that if *we* ever make love, it *will* be different.'

It took a moment or two for her to process what he'd said, but when her head lifted and she finally looked straight at him with those beautiful turquoise eyes, there was an expression in them that he'd never seen before.

'Show me,' she said, and while her voice still trembled, there was a new strength to it, an air of decision.

'Show you what?' He needed her to spell out exactly what she meant before he jumped the gun and ruined everything.

Her chin inched up just a fraction and he couldn't have felt more proud of her if she'd just won a Nobel prize. 'Show me how different it is to make love,' she said, and this time there was clear determination in her voice.

'Nadia, are you sure?' His body was screaming at him to take her at her word but his heart and brain were urging caution. 'This isn't just because you feel you ought to…because we're married?'

'No,' she said bluntly, the single decisive shake of her head sending shards of light glimmering over her beautiful blonde hair. 'This is because I love you and…and even though we have been sharing your flat, and you have asked me to marry you, and you have been so kind and patient and never pushed for me to do anything… Oh!' she gasped as a sudden thought struck her. 'Perhaps that is because…because you don't want me *that* way?'

Gideon gave a wry chuckle, remembering the weeks of discomfort he'd gone through even while he'd revelled in sharing his bed with her. 'Oh, Nadia, you don't ever have to doubt that I want you,' he said. 'But I would never want you to feel that…'

He was silenced by the soft brush of her fingers on his mouth. 'Hush, Gideon. I *know* I can trust you to keep your word. That isn't the problem. It's…the thought of having *that* happen to me, ever again, that makes me feel so scared. Every time, I felt so power-less…so vulnerable…'

He could see the dark memories in the shadows in her eyes and ached for the innocent girl she'd once been. Then she continued in a very different voice. '*But* I also know that I want something more than just holding you. I want to know if there can really be pleasure in some-thing so…so violent…so demeaning…so—'

'Hey,' he interrupted quickly, relieving her of her cup to distract her from that train of thought. 'That bad stuff is all in the past. From now on, you're going to be making new memories…*good* memories, with me.'

Tension was still thrumming through her, almost loud enough to hear over the sound of a passing emergency

siren, and he sent up a silent prayer that he would be able
to fulfil his promises.

'So…' He briskly stripped off his scrub top, making her
blink, then shuffled back on the bed and lay down, spreading himself out like a sacrificial victim. 'I'm all yours. Do
your worst…but be gentle with me. I bruise easily.'

Nadia almost laughed at his deliberate nonsense, and
he could see that her eyes were flickering over the bared
expanse of his chest, but at least she now looked intrigued instead of just scared.

'What do you want me to do?' she asked, and the first
answer that leapt into his head was definitely X-rated.

'Whatever you want to,' he said when he'd managed to
slap his over-eager imagination down. 'It's your choice.'

'But…' Suddenly, she looked lost and he silently cursed
himself for making her feel the slightest bit inadequate.

'How about starting off with a bit of exploration?' he
suggested. 'You don't often come across a body as magnificent as mine, so you may as well take advantage of
the opportunity.' He waggled teasing eyebrows.

That startled a chuckle out of her. 'Magnificent?'

He shrugged in mock modesty. 'What can I tell you?
I was just born lucky, so if you want to feel a few
muscles, test them for size and strength…you know, do
a thorough scientific evaluation…' He reached across
for her hand and placed it on his biceps before pumping
the muscle like a bodybuilder. 'Good, eh?'

She left her hand where he'd placed it for several
seconds, passively, but then he felt the slight quiver in
her fingers as she pressed them, oh, so briefly into the
muscle before she hurriedly took it away again.

He almost groaned aloud, wondering if that was as

far as she was going to go. Had she been too badly trau-
matised to ever be able to venture any further?

Slowly and deliberately he tucked both hands behind
his head, not just so that he couldn't do what he wanted
to do—wrap her in his arms until there wasn't a fraction
of an atom separating the two of them—but also to send
the signal to her that she didn't have to be afraid that he
would grab her and force her to his will.

For several long seconds it almost felt as if the world
stood still while her eyes travelled from his face to his
naked chest then back again and he found himself
holding his breath while she came to her decision.

Then, when one tentative hand reached out and
trembling fingertips tested the curling dark hair
circling his nipple, he felt like bursting out into the
'Hallelujah Chorus'.

It was torture, lying there, forcing himself not to
move a muscle while she traced the dark swathe across
his chest and probed the flat discs of his nipples, and he
nearly whimpered aloud when they tightened into hard
points in response and her mouth opened in surprise.

'That response works for both of us,' he murmured
in a voice that held a distinct hint of a growl. 'If you ever
want a demonstration…?' he offered, only just remembering to waggle his eyebrows again to rob his words
of any hint that he was pushing her.

Even so, she stiffened, her hands freezing for a
moment in their ministrations while she glanced down
in wonder at the similar evidence pushing against the
silky fabric of her nightdress.

'Oh!' she breathed with evident delight, and Gideon
wondered if it was possible to die of anticipation. Then

he saw the sudden spark of determination in her eyes, and as she slid both hands over his chest and down he was glad he'd spent the time resurrecting the six-pack he'd all but lost during the endless days and nights of his medical training.

His heart thumped when she reached the drawstring top of the scrubs he'd been using as pyjamas for the last few weeks, and he knew she couldn't help but see the way the thin cotton fabric was tented by his body's eager response.

'My body can't do *that*,' she murmured with a pointed glance.

'No, but your body *causes* that, every time you walk in a room… Hell, it even happens when I walk into the bathroom and smell your shampoo,' he grumbled. He was secretly delighted to see a new gleam in her eyes and that made him bold enough to add, 'Your own body responds, too, even if it isn't in such an obvious way.'

'How?' she demanded. 'What sort of response?'

For the sake of his sanity, he tried to keep the discussion clinical, knowing that she would have learned most of the details during her training, but he could tell that she was cataloguing every word he spoke against what she was experiencing, and it was killing him to lie there with his fingers clenched in his hair, pretending that he was unaffected.

'Gideon,' she interrupted, and the sight of her eyes so darkly dilated with arousal dried all the moisture from his mouth even as it turned his insides to water. 'I think…' There was a quiver in her voice that could have been nervousness or excitement—or both. 'I think we might be wearing too many clothes,' she suggested, and when she reached unsteady hands to the hem of her nightdress he was unable to utter a single word to ask her if she was certain before she was pulling it over her head.

'Nadia…' His voice was a croak while he tried to voice how unutterably beautiful she was, with the light from the en suite highlighting every sensual curve and making each hollow into a dark mystery that begged investigation. Then she reached for the ties at his waist and he could do nothing more than watch her fumble with the knot he'd tied until she could spread the opening wide.

'Help me?' she asked, and he complied gently, desperate not to do anything to dent her new-found bravery and hoping desperately that she would have the courage to take events all the way to their natural conclusion.

His heart was beating so loudly in his ears that he almost missed her next question.

'Is this all right?' she whispered as she shyly positioned herself so that she could settle one knee on either side of his hips.

'Oh, yes!' he groaned, and the feel of the silky skin of her pale thighs against his and the sight of her poised over him was enough to have him silently subtracting seven from one thousand over and over again so that he didn't explode.

'And this?' she asked, as she reached one hand to position him at her entrance and made contact between their bodies.

'Anything, Nadia,' he told her hoarsely, knowing that

his desperation must be clear in his voice. 'You can do anything you want.' And to his utter relief she wanted the same thing he did; to join their bodies together for the first time; to voluntarily take him deep inside her body in an act of love.

'You were right,' Nadia admitted when she could breathe again, her body spread-eagled bonelessly over the top of Gideon's with his arms wrapped around her to hold her in position.

'Of course I was,' he said smugly, his voice rumbling around in his chest under her ear. 'I'm always right,' he added, and when he arched his hips, she realised that he was still fully aroused and still buried deep inside her body.

The fact that the realisation sent a spear of renewed desire through her was definitely something new, as was the way her own muscles tightened in response.

In fact, everything had been so different from anything she'd known before that she had questions she wanted to ask…things she needed to know…

'I can hear your brain whirring,' he said softly, and she lifted her head up in time to see an unexpected look of uncertainty on his face.

Gideon? Uncertain? That was a new thought. She'd been convinced that she was the only one who'd been filled with doubts and insecurity.

'Speak to me,' he prompted, and the tension had crept into his voice now. 'Do you regret what we've done? The marriage? This? Would you rather—?'

'No!' she gasped, pushing herself up with both hands on his chest so that she could look fully down into his face. Concentrating so hard on setting his mind at rest, she only peripherally noticed that the change in position prompted her newly sensitised tissues to want more.

'I don't regret anything, Gideon, especially not *this*.' She glanced down at the point where the two of them were joined, hoping her embarrassment didn't look as obvious as it felt.

'Then what *is* the matter?' he demanded patiently, his hands moving gently up and down her arms as though he was soothing a frightened animal.

The way he was looking at her, pleasure in what he was seeing clear in his face, was so flattering that she nearly forgot what she wanted to ask.

'It's nothing, really. Just…' She dragged in a quivering breath, silently cursing her ignorance. 'Is it always like that?' she demanded in a rush, afraid that he was going to laugh at her lack of knowledge. 'Is it always like…like the biggest firework in the world exploding inside you, but instead of blowing you apart, it makes you feel as if you become part of each other, so you don't know where one person ends and the other one begins?'

'Only if a couple is very, very lucky,' he said fervently, a heated glow seeming to radiate from those beautiful green eyes.

He arched his hips again, and when she realised that he was watching intently for her reaction, this time she countered the move, deliberately pressing her body down on his.

'Oh, yes!' he breathed, and she could see from the pulse at the base of his throat that his heart was starting to beat as fast as her own. 'Definitely lucky,' he said as he gently rolled her until they were lying side by side, and she realised that in this position neither of them would be dominating the other.

For just a second she was still, probing her feelings and finding that all the old terrors were gone in the arms of the one man she knew she could trust.

'I've a feeling we're about to get luckier, Gideon,' she said as she deliberately rolled onto her back, pulling him so that he was on top of her, then wrapping her legs around him to hold him in position when he would have lifted himself away from her.

Experimentally, she arched her hips and the result was so pleasurable that she felt a wide smile creeping over her face, a smile that only grew wider when he thrust deep in return.

'In fact,' she murmured distractedly as she gave herself over to delight she'd never dreamed of, 'I think our good luck is going to last for the rest of our lives.'

2 FREE

BOOKS AND A SURPRISE GIFT!

We would like to take this opportunity to thank you for reading this Mills & Boon® book by offering you the chance to take TWO more specially selected titles from the Medical™ series absolutely FREE! We're also making this offer to introduce you to the benefits of the Mills & Boon® Book Club™—

- ★ **FREE home delivery**
- ★ **FREE gifts and competitions**
- ★ **FREE monthly Newsletter**
- ★ **Exclusive Mills & Boon Book Club offers**
- ★ **Books available before they're in the shops**

Accepting these FREE books and gift places you under no obligation to buy, you may cancel at any time, even after receiving your free shipment. Simply complete your details below and return the entire page to the address below. You don't even need a stamp!

YES! Please send me 2 free Medical books and a surprise gift. I understand that unless you hear from me, I will receive 4 superb new titles every month for just £2.99 each, postage and packing free. I am under no obligation to purchase any books and may cancel my subscription at any time. The free books and gift will be mine to keep in any case.

M9ZED

Ms/Mrs/Miss/Mr ....Initials ....
BLOCK CAPITALS PLEASE

Surname ....

Address ....

....

....Postcode.........................

Send this whole page to:
UK: FREEPOST CN8I, Croydon, CR9 3WZ